LOVE IS TRIUMPHANT

In his eagerness he had seized her hands and was holding them tightly. There was a burning light in his eyes as he looked at her, and she could feel his warm breath fanning her face.

Startled, Rosina gazed back at him so that their eyes met and she seemed to be looking directly into his soul. At the same time she had a disconcerting feeling that he too was looking into her soul.

She took fright. How dare he do this, as though every thought and feeling she had was opened up to him. How dare he understand her!

She snatched her hands back, turning away from him.

"Forgive me," he said. "I didn't mean to – what you do is none of my business."

"Indeed it is not," she said in a shaking voice.

"I wish you every success, Miss Clarendon. You deserve the best that the world has to offer."

Without warning she found herself on the verge of tears. She took a moment to control herself, then turned back to smile at him, wanting to be friends again.

But he had gone.

THE BARBARA CARTLAND PINK COLLECTION

Titles in this series

LOVE IS TRIUMPHANT

BARBARA CARTLAND

Barbaracartland.com Ltd

THE BARBARA CARTLAND PINK COLLECTION

Barbara Cartland was the most prolific bestselling author in the history of the world. She was frequently in the Guinness Book of Records for writing more books in a year than any other living author. In fact her most amazing literary feat was when her publishers asked for more Barbara Cartland romances, she doubled her output from 10 books a year to over 20 books a year, when she was 77.

She went on writing continuously at this rate for 20 years and wrote her last book at the age of 97, thus completing 400 books between the ages of 77 and 97.

Her publishers finally could not keep up with this phenomenal output, so at her death she left 160 unpublished manuscripts, something again that no other author has ever achieved.

Now the exciting news is that these 160 original unpublished Barbara Cartland books are already being published and by Barbaracartland.com exclusively on the internet, as the international web is the best possible way of reaching so many Barbara Cartland readers around the world.

The 160 books are published monthly and will be numbered in sequence.

The series is called the Pink Collection as a tribute to Barbara Cartland whose favourite colour was pink and it became very much her trademark over the years.

The Barbara Cartland Pink Collection is published only on the internet. Log on to www.barbaracartland.com to find out how you can purchase the books monthly as they are published, and take out a subscription that will ensure that all subsequent editions are delivered to you by mail order to your home.

NEW

Barbaracartland.com is proud to announce the publication of ten new Audio Books for the first time as CDs. They are favourite Barbara Cartland stories read by well-known actors and actresses and each story extends to 4 or 5 CDs. The Audio Books are as follows :

The Patient Bridegroom	The Passion and the Flower
A Challenge of Hearts	Little White Doves of Love
A Train to Love	The Prince and the Pekinese
The Unbroken Dream	A King in Love
The Cruel Count	A Sign of Love

More Audio Books will be published in the future and the above titles can be purchased by logging on to the website www.barbaracartland.com or please write to the address below.

If you do not have access to a computer, you can write for information about the Barbara Cartland Pink Collection and the Barbara Cartland Audio Books to the following address :

Barbara Cartland.com Ltd.
Camfield Place,
Hatfield,
Hertfordshire AL9 6JE
United Kingdom.
Telephone: +44 (0)1707 642629
Fax: +44 (0)1707 663041

THE LATE DAME BARBARA CARTLAND

Barbara Cartland who sadly died in May 2000 at the age of nearly 99 was the world's most famous romantic novelist who wrote 723 books in her lifetime with worldwide sales of over 1 billion copies and her books were translated into 36 different languages.

As well as romantic novels, she wrote historical biographies, 6 autobiographies, theatrical plays, books of advice on life, love, vitamins and cookery. She also found time to be a political speaker and television and radio personality.

She wrote her first book at the age of 21 and this was called Jigsaw. It became an immediate bestseller and sold 100,000 copies in hardback and was translated into 6 different languages. She wrote continuously throughout her life, writing bestsellers for an astonishing 76 years. Her books have always been immensely popular in the United States, where in 1976 her current books were at numbers 1 & 2 in the B. Dalton bestsellers list, a feat never achieved before or since by any author.

Barbara Cartland became a legend in her own lifetime and will be best remembered for her wonderful romantic novels, so loved by her millions of readers throughout the world.

Her books will always be treasured for their moral message, her pure and innocent heroines, her good looking and dashing heroes and above all her belief that the power of love is more important than anything else in everyone's life.

"Everyone falls in love at least once in a lifetime, and it is always a unique, wonderful and spiritual experience."

Barbara Cartland

CHAPTER ONE
1868

Rosina Clarendon was lying on her bed, reading a book, when there was a knock on her door.

"The Headmistress would like to see you, miss," said the maid who carried messages throughout the school.

Rosina checked herself in the mirror to make sure she was not untidy and found her appearance neat enough to please even the eagle-eyed Miss Baxter.

She could not think why the Head had sent for her, but she had no fear of being in trouble. As the daughter of Sir Elroy Clarendon, the local Member of Parliament, she was a privileged person. She was given special treatment in many ways at Laine Hall, including a bedroom to herself, some distance away from the dormitories where the other girls slept.

She tried never to take advantage of this favouritism, but she was not surprised when she entered Miss Baxter's study and was greeted by a smile.

"There you are, Rosina. I only sent for you because you have a visitor. Sir John Crosby has come to call on you on behalf of your distinguished father."

The name of Sir John took her by surprise and for a

moment it was hard to control the impulse to smile with pleasure. He was a handsome young man and she had enjoyed many sweet dreams about him, dreams that he knew nothing about.

"Sir John Crosby?" she said innocently. "I wonder why he is here."

"He will tell you himself," Miss Baxter said, rising from behind her desk. "He's standing just behind you."

Rosina whirled round and saw Sir John's laughing face.

"Why I – I didn't see you," she stammered.

She had a horrid suspicion that she was blushing as though all her thoughts about him might be written on her face. But she managed to greet him with an appearance of composure.

"Has something happened to Papa or Mama?" she asked anxiously. "Is it bad news?"

"Not at all. All is well with your family, but I just happened to be passing through on my way to my constituency and volunteered to bring you some letters from your parents."

"How kind of you," she exclaimed.

He turned to the Headmistress, giving her his most charming smile.

"Miss Baxter, I am sure it's against the rules, but may I speak alone with Miss Clarendon?"

"Well – " Miss Baxter hesitated, conscious that Rosina was no longer a child and would be a *debutante* very soon.

"Perhaps we could take a walk in the gardens," Sir John persisted. "If we promise not to move out of sight from the house."

"In that case – yes. I am sure you understand, Sir

John, that we have to be very careful with such an attractive young lady, about to emerge into Society – "

"Of course I do and you may trust me to protect her reputation."

Just how could any woman resist his smile, Rosina wondered, or the warmth of his demeanour, or the vibrancy in his voice, or his way of looking and sounding as though life was a fruit to be devoured, and he was going to enjoy all of it?

Apparently the Headmistress could not resist it either.

"Then you may go into the garden," she said. "But not for too long."

Demurely Rosina walked beside Sir John into the sunny garden, trying not to look too pleased at being with him.

'Don't be silly,' she admonished herself severely. 'To him you are just a schoolgirl.'

In a short time she would be eighteen, and ready for her 'coming out' ball. Then she would wear pink and white satin with rosebuds in her hair and her mother's pearls about her neck.

How grown-up she would look! In her happy dream she was a glorious vision with her fair hair and deep blue eyes, her tall, slim figure and glowing, peachy complexion. And Sir John, who would naturally be at the ball, would be struck dumb with love at the sight of her.

She pictured him gazing, enraptured, as she made her grand entrance, wondering why he had never noticed this staggering beauty before.

But that was for the future, she thought wistfully. For the moment she was trapped in a school uniform of blue serge that reduced her figure to a flat board. Instead of being swept up in a glamorous coiffure, her hair was worn down and held back by a ribbon.

3

"We'll just go as far as the stream," said Sir John. "We'll still be in sight of the building."

If only he would grab her hand and run into the woods, she mused. If only he wanted to be alone with her – to steal a kiss.

But evidently he wanted no such thing, so she merely nodded and said,

"What a good idea!"

There was a fallen log by the stream and since the weather was fine and dry they were able to sit on it.

"Things are humming in London, as you can imagine," Sir John began.

"Well, I know that the Prime Minister, Mr. Disraeli, was defeated over some bill," Rosina said. "So there's going to have to be a general election and Papa is very excited about it, because he thinks he may actually be a Minister in the next Government. But I only know that because he wrote and told me so himself. We aren't expected to read newspapers here."

"I'm very sure you don't obey that prohibition," added Sir John with a twinkle.

"Certainly not. I buy some in the village and Miss Draycott lets me read hers. But don't tell anyone or she might get into trouble."

"Who is Miss Draycott?"

"The music mistress. She's quite young and very nice."

"You mean she isn't scandalised by your unfeminine interest in politics?" he teased.

"Seeing as Papa is an MP, she is understanding about it. Besides, the man she loves is also in politics or at least, he intends to be."

"Good Heavens! Who?"

But Rosina shook her head.

"I can't tell you that. It isn't my secret. I shouldn't even have told you her name and I wouldn't have done so if I had been thinking properly. Please forget it."

"Very well. But I hope for her sake that this man has money."

"He hasn't," answered Rosina.

"Then just what are they planning to live on?" he demanded. "Even if he secures a seat in Parliament, he will not be paid. MPs don't get a salary, so he will need another job. Perhaps he's a lawyer or something like that?"

Rosina's father was a very successful lawyer who, for years, had combined a prosperous legal practice with sitting in the House of Commons. Sir John himself was a wealthy landowner who did not need to earn money.

"He isn't a lawyer," said Rosina now with a sigh. "He meant to be, but he failed his bar exams. His health was poor at the time," she added hastily, "and so it wasn't his fault."

"It makes no difference whose fault it was," replied Sir John firmly. "The fact is that he has no income and no means of earning one without passing his exams. Can he take them again?"

Rosina shook her head.

"He failed very badly. They told him not to return."

"Wealthy relatives?"

"His uncle makes him a modest allowance, but is growing cross with him."

"I am not surprised. He sounds a feeble character."

"That is most unfair," flared Rosina. "How can you, who have never been ill or poor, understand his situation?"

He looked at her curiously.

"I thought it was Miss Draycott who was in love with him, not you."

5

"How dare you say such a thing. I have never even met him."

"Forgive me. I shouldn't have said that."

"No, you shouldn't," she said furiously.

She could never understand why she always seemed to end up at odds with Sir John. When he was absent, she dreamed about his handsome face. When he was present, she noticed only how infuriating he could be.

"Let's forget my sins," he said in a voice that was almost placating, "and return to this man and how he is to obtain a good income so that he can marry your friend. Not that I think any right-minded woman would want to tie herself to such a – all right, all right," he added hastily, reading retribution in her eyes.

"Perhaps he will find a wealthy patron," suggested Rosina, controlling herself with difficulty.

"Has he found one so far?"

"I don't think so."

"Then he'll have to marry money."

"What a dreadful thing to say," Rosina flared up again.

"My dear girl, I am only trying to alert you to the dangers. If this lady you seem so fond of, is hoping this man will marry her, both you and she should be warned that it is very unlikely."

"But they love each other," she cried. "You should see the words he writes in his letters."

"I'd like to," said Sir John, a touch grimly. "He sounds like a cad to me."

"You know nothing about him," Rosina came back angrily. "He loves her truly, devotedly, passionately – "

"Enough to give up his ambition? Because he will have to if he cannot find enough financial backing from somewhere."

"It will not come to that. They *will* marry and he *will* find a patron – "

"And a good fairy will appear and wave her magic wand and they'll live happily ever after," Sir John came back impatiently. "My dear child, you're living in a romantic fantasy. The real world is a harsh place and I am afraid your friend is going to be hurt."

"I've told you, they love each other," she insisted firmly.

"Oh – love," he replied dismissively.

"Why must you sneer?"

"I am not sneering, but I think we load far too many burdens onto 'love', most of which it's ill-equipped to bear. Love is very sweet for a time, but the man who relies on it is a fool."

An edge of bitterness had crept into his voice. Rosina stared at him.

"But we were talking about a woman," she said slowly.

He seemed to recover himself.

"Man or woman, it makes very little difference," he responded quickly. "There is love and there is reality and it is better not to confuse the two."

Rosina was now silent, astonished at this unexpected glimpse he had given her into his own experience. For a moment there had been real pain in his voice.

"I don't think you should assume that everyone's experience has been like yours," she said carefully.

"Like mine?" he repeated sharply. "What are you talking about? We weren't talking about me."

"I think we were."

"Don't be so dashed impertinent!" he said angrily. "At your age, what do you know about anything?"

"I know when a man's talking about himself – "

"My dear child – "

"And stop talking to me like that," she fumed. "I am not a child, I am not yours and I have no desire to be your *dear* anything."

"I feel exactly the same. A prickly, naggy creature like yourself is the last girl I would ever – you should start being a little careful how you speak to men, Rosina. When you're a *debutante* you'll want them to like you and they won't like you if you're always wiping your feet on them, the way you do with me."

"Some men positively beg to have a woman's feet wiped on them," she snapped. "And then they have only themselves to blame."

"I take it I am included in that list?" he asked, his eyes kindling.

"Should you be?"

For a moment she thought he would explode. Then he turned away, raised his fists into the air and roared up into the sky.

"Heaven give me patience! I pity the man who marries you, Rosina. He will never get a word in edgeways."

"Which will save me from having to listen to a lot of nonsense," she replied tartly.

"On second thoughts, you are plainly destined to be an old maid."

"That will suit me very well."

For a moment the silence was sulphurous. Then he sighed and came back to sit beside her, his good humour restored.

"However did we start exchanging pleasantries?" he asked, taking her hand. "I did not mean to be unkind about Miss Draycott, only to utter a friendly warning."

"I know," she sighed. "I'm sorry. It's just that the whole thing is so unfair. MPs ought to be paid and then he could win a seat and they could afford to marry."

"The idea is to make sure that they are all wealthy enough to be independent," Sir John explained. "It keeps out men who are regarded as 'not good enough'."

"That's *outrageous*."

"I agree and one day it will have to be changed. People like your father and myself are working for changes. So is our leader, Mr. Gladstone. That is why it's so important that the Liberals win the coming election. But I am afraid it won't be in time to do this couple any good."

"They ought to give women the vote," said Rosina crossly. "In fact they ought to let us sit in Parliament."

"Well, maybe that too will happen one day," he soothed.

"Are you daring to patronise me?" she demanded, ready to be angry again.

"I wouldn't dare. You scare me. You are the most terrifyingly intelligent young woman I know."

Inwardly she sighed. So much for now dreaming of dazzling him with her beauty. She was intelligent. She terrified him.

"I cannot help being intelligent."

"Not only intelligent but well-informed."

"Which is another crime in a woman," she reminded him.

"With your background you could hardly be anything else. I think your father was already in Parliament when you were born, wasn't he?"

"Yes, he won his seat in '46 and I was born four years later. I hardly saw Papa on my second birthday because it coincided with election night. And nobody ever talked about anything else but politics in our house and Uncle William is Papa's friend."

The man she so casually referred to as 'Uncle William' was in fact William Ewart Gladstone, leader of the Liberal Party.

"And 'Uncle William' will win the coming election and be Prime Minister," Sir John supplied. "At least, that is what we must all hope and work for. He is a great man, a great reformer. He sees what's wrong with this country and he thinks – "

'Oh, Heavens!' thought Rosina. 'This is not what I want to hear at this moment.'

But she could see that Sir John was now fired with enthusiasm, and she didn't want to say or do anything that would bring the time with him to an end – even if he was the most annoying man she had ever known. So she listened carefully and made intelligent observations and at last he told her,

"It was nice of you to listen to me. I have managed to get several ideas sorted out in my head."

"I am so glad," she said politely.

Inwardly she sighed again. She would much rather he told her that she was pretty and her eyes were like stars.

But later, she promised herself. Later. When she was eighteen.

"I cannot wait to leave school," she said, "and be part of all the excitement."

"It is going to be an exciting time," he agreed. "Here are the letters from your parents. I think you will find they have a lot to say about plans for the summer. Your mother told me you were all thinking of going to Italy."

"Oh, I'm sure that's all off now," she said cheerfully. "Who could possibly want to go to Italy, when they could get pelted on the hustings instead?"

"That's the spirit," he told her, clapping her heartily on the shoulder. "Well, I must be going now. I dare say we'll bump into each other again during the course of the election campaign."

"I am sure we will," she assured him politely.

'Otherwise,' she thought, 'you won't give me another thought until the Liberals have won. And then you will probably have a Government job and think of me even less.'

As they walked back to the school building they came in sight of the wing where Rosina had her room, two floors up. Looking up she saw Miss Draycott standing on the balcony outside her window. The teacher waved cheerfully when she saw Rosina and pointed to the watch on her wrist.

"That's Miss Draycott," Rosina told Sir John. "She's reminding me that I have a music lesson with her in about five minutes."

"Then I will leave you here. Please say goodbye to the Headmistress for me."

He gave her a little bow and departed.

Rosina looked up towards Miss Draycott on the high balcony, waved back and began to hurry into the building.

Miss Draycott was not like the other teachers. She was very pretty and only about twenty-five. Her room was next door to Rosina's and it had been easy for them to become close friends.

Gradually the age gap between them had seemed to vanish and at last Miss Draycott had confided in Rosina about the man she loved. His name was Arthur Woodward and he was ambitious to enter politics and climb to the top.

To the young Rosina the whole story was wildly romantic. More thrilling still was being allowed to read some of his letters with their expressions of love and passion.

'Oh, how I hope that someday a wonderful man will write to me like this,' she fantasised.

At that moment she was not thinking particularly of Sir John. She enjoyed the mild, exciting infatuation she felt for him, but she knew it was not the overwhelming love that she hoped to find some day.

When that day came, it seemed to her that to receive such declarations of devotion must be the pinnacle of any woman's life.

Certainly Miss Draycott seemed to feel the same. There was a glow about her today that Rosina thought she understood.

"Has he written again?" she whispered and the teacher nodded joyfully.

There were three other girls taking the lesson, so they were unable to talk further. Later Rosina had a geography lesson, but as soon as it was over she raced upstairs and knocked on Miss Draycott's door.

"Come in."

She entered to find the teacher standing in the tall window that led out onto the balcony. She had a letter clutched in her hand and looked ecstatically happy.

"And who was that good-looking young man I saw you with?" she teased.

"Oh, you mean Sir John Crosby?" Rosina replied with a shrug. "He's not particularly good-looking."

"Isn't he?"

"Anyway, how could you tell from here? It's too far away."

Miss Draycott laughed.

"I could tell by the way you seemed so absorbed in him."

"I was *not*," replied Rosina stung.

She looked right down at the ground, at the stones immediately beneath them, then the lawns leading to the woods and the stream. For a moment the height made her giddy.

"Come back from the edge," Miss Draycott warned. "These balcony rails are not quite high enough for tall women like us."

They drew back into the room and closed the window.

"What did Mr. Woodward have to say?" asked Rosina.

"He's taking me out tonight. We're going to eat at a smart restaurant." She indicated two dresses hanging up, one blue, one pink. "Which of these do you think I should wear?"

"Oh, I think the pink one."

"Yes, I am sure that Arthur will admire me in pink as I wore blue when I dined with him last week."

"Mind you," remarked Rosina, "I don't think he'll mind what you wear. Not if he really loves you."

"Oh, he *does* love me, I know he does," said Miss Draycott at once. "And I love him with all my heart. I am hoping and praying that he will ask me to be his wife."

"How thrilling that will be," enthused Rosina. "When he's in Parliament you will have to have a house in London. Then there will be parties and theatres and all sorts of nice things to go to every night. It will be very exciting."

Miss Draycott smiled.

"It will be glorious just to be with the man I love and who loves me," she answered.

She spoke very softly, as if she was speaking to herself.

Rosina was silent for a moment. She could not help thinking of Sir John's warning that Miss Draycott's lover would either need a wealthy patron or a wealthy wife.

But he loved her, Rosina reassured herself. What could ambition matter beside true love?

Miss Draycott was sighing happily, lost in the vision of herself as a bride.

"I think I will have my wedding dress made up in London," she said. "After all, the wedding is the most important day of a woman's life. I want my husband to remember me as being more beautiful than at any other time we have been together."

"I'm sure he'll think so."

Miss Draycott sighed.

"I only wish I was rich. Then I could help Arthur in all sorts of ways."

"Perhaps he'll win some money racing or a relation will die and leave you a fortune," suggested Rosina.

Miss Draycott spoke with sudden bitterness.

"That only happens in books. In real life you struggle to keep your head above water, but without money you are likely to sink to the bottom and no one will even be sorry for you."

Then she brightened again, for nothing could depress her for long when she was going to meet the man she adored.

"Would you like to see his letter?" she asked eagerly.

Rosina took the letter that had arrived that very day and read,

'*I will count the hours until we are together tonight. Unfortunately I have to go away tomorrow to visit some friends, but I'll just start counting the hours again until I can see you.*

'*I am longing to see you tonight and to tell you how much I love you. That will take me a very long time. Goodbye, my darling, and think of me until we meet.*'

"That is so lovely," murmured Rosina. "It's the sort of

letter I would like someone to write to me."

"It will soon be your turn," said Miss Draycott.

"You must keep such a beautiful letter."

"Of course I will keep it. I keep all Arthur's letters and when I feel depressed and miserable, I read them over and over again."

Rosina helped her to finish dressing and waved her off. When it was time to go to bed that night she lay awake, thinking of her friend and how madly in love she was.

Then she thought of Sir John and heard again the sudden bitterness in his voice when he spoke of love.

What had he meant by it?

Had he been in love with some girl who had not loved him in return?

She was suddenly aware that he had a whole life that was hidden from her. In reality she knew almost nothing about him.

She wondered what her own lover would be like and when he would arrive in her life. Would he be charming, handsome and passionately devoted to her?

She tried to picture him on one knee before her, offering his heart and a diamond ring.

But all she could see was Sir John glaring at her and calling her a silly child.

She turned over and thumped the pillow in frustration.

CHAPTER TWO

As the night wore on Rosina's thoughts strayed more and more to Miss Draycott and her lover. What was happening now? Had he proposed? Were they celebrating their future happiness?

She had once seen them together, although even Miss Draycott did not know about that. She had been buying some oddments in the village, accompanied by a couple of the other pupils, for girls were not allowed to go to the village alone.

They had been thinking of going into a teashop and Rosina had looked inside one as they passed. There she had seen Miss Draycott and a very handsome young man, sitting together in the corner, absorbed in each other.

Arthur Woodward had been smiling in a way that added greatly to his looks. But it had been Miss Draycott herself who held Rosina's attention.

The way she held her lover's hand, the fervour with which she gazed at him, above all her total, enraptured stillness, all these pointers showed Rosina that this was a woman in the grip of a death defying passion.

This man was her life, her world. She wanted no other and could have no other. Without him there would be nothing.

As for him, he was surely devoting himself to her

charmingly, but he was not lost in her as she was lost in him. The chasm between what he felt for her and what she felt for him appeared very plain.

Rosina had turned away suddenly to face the girls with her.

"Not this place," she told them. "I don't like it."

"But we want some tea," they had protested.

"We must find somewhere else," she had said firmly, determined to protect Miss Draycott from prying eyes.

She had meant to tell Miss Draycott what she had seen and they could smile about it together. But strangely she found that she could not speak about it. She had seen something she had not been meant to see, something deeply private and secret. And she knew she must keep silent.

But she could never forget what she had witnessed. Now she knew how a woman looked when she loved a man body and soul, more than her own life, so that nothing but him existed in the whole world.

The intensity of it was almost frightening.

All this came back to her as she lay listening for Miss Draycott's return. When at last it came she knew there had been no proposal.

Her friend walked very slowly as though there were a heaviness in her heart and something about that sound warned Rosina not to go to her, but to leave her to grieve in private.

*

Over the days that followed Rosina found that although Miss Draycott was meeting her lover on every possible occasion, there were long days and nights when she did not see him.

But the letters arrived almost every morning.

They kept her happy even though Rosina was well

17

aware that the future seemed inevitably dark and empty, since he never mentioned marriage.

'If I could see him,' thought Rosina, 'I would tell him that he should marry Miss Draycott and somehow they would manage together to make some money, however difficult it may seem now.'

Then one night when Rosina was undressing and getting ready for bed, she heard someone drive up to their wing.

Looking down from her window she saw a man slip a letter through the letter box. It was hard to see clearly from this height and in the darkness, but she could almost have sworn that the man was Arthur Woodward.

But why was he delivering his letter in such a secretive way and at this time of night?

Throwing on her dressing gown, Rosina hurried downstairs. There lay the letter on the mat and it was addressed to Miss Draycott.

She snatched it up and hurried back upstairs.

As she reached the hall Miss Draycott opened her door.

"Where have you been at this hour?" she asked.

"Collecting something which has just been delivered for you," answered Rosina, holding out the envelope.

"Just been delivered!" exclaimed Miss Draycott.

She took the letter and returned to her room, Rosina following her.

"How strange, that he should write to me at such a late hour. His letters usually arrive in the morning."

She lit the lamp and Rosina could see that her eyes were shining.

"It must be something very special," she mused. "Something that couldn't wait. Oh, Rosina, do you think –

after all this time – ?"

"Perhaps. Read it quickly."

"Don't go. Stay a moment, and then I can share the good news with you. Then you can go to bed and sleep happily as I will do."

Rosina smiled at her.

"I must admit I am rather curious," she said, "as to what is in that envelope."

It would have been truer to say that she was full of foreboding. Something told her that all was not well.

Miss Draycott sat down on the bed, took out the letter and started to read it.

Rosina did not move or say anything. She just waited, her eyes fixed on her friend's face.

As Miss Draycott read the first page, then turned it over to read the second, asked Rosina in a low voice,

"Is it good news?"

Miss Draycott did not answer.

Then as she finished reading, she folded up the letter.

Putting it on her lap, she stared at the wall as if she was seeing something.

She did not speak.

As the minutes passed, Rosina asked gently,

"What has happened?"

For a moment Miss Draycott did not reply.

Then she said in a voice which did not sound like her own,

"Well, we were both partly correct. This letter is to announce his intention to marry – but not to *me*."

"I don't believe it," muttered Rosina mechanically.

But in the depths of her heart, she knew that she did believe it. Sir John had been right all the time and suddenly she hated him for it.

"He has considered the matter," said Miss Draycott slowly, "and believes that we have no future together. He wants – " she broke off and a shudder went through her, "he wants me to return all his letters."

"Who is he marrying?" asked Rosina in a tight voice.

"He does not say." Miss Draycott gave a forlorn smile. "Perhaps he is afraid that if I knew I would make trouble. He need not worry. I would do nothing to harm him. I hope he'll be very happy and have everything he wants in life."

She spoke in a soft heart-broken voice that filled Rosina with dread. Following dread came anger.

"I hope he won't be happy," she snarled through gritted teeth. "I hope he'll be as miserable as he deserves to be."

"Don't say that," Miss Draycott replied fiercely to her. "Don't wish him ill. I forbid you, do you understand?"

"But why should he be happy when he has treated you like this?" Rosina cried. "What right does he have?"

"Every right. If he finds he cannot love me then – then he is right to leave me. He can be a great man, a politician, a leader, and he must let nothing stand in his way. If I must stand aside for his welfare then – then I am willing to do so."

"But the way he's treated you – "

"He has done what he had to," Miss Draycott added in a shaking voice, "and I honour him for it. He will suffer no harm or scandal because of me."

She turned a ravaged face on Rosina.

"Don't you understand?" she implored in a husky voice. "To do him no harm is all I can hope for."

"How can you say that?" cried Rosina. "He's a greedy selfish coward. Why don't you hate him?"

"Because I love him. Even now I love him. I cannot help it. One day you will love a man more than your own life and love him so much that your own welfare means nothing as long as you can do him some good. When that day comes, you will understand."

"I hope I never feel like that," Rosina told her bitterly. "If love makes a slave of a woman, then I hope I never feel it."

"I pity you if you never know love."

"If I never know love, I shall never know pain," responded Rosina in a hard voice.

"And you will never know glory. Now, if you don't mind, I would like to be quite alone."

Her voice was now no longer shaking, but firm and decided.

Rosina had no choice but to do as she wished.

In the doorway she stopped and looked back. Miss Draycott was still standing there with her back to her.

"Remember," said Rosina, "I am always your friend. I will do anything you wish."

"Thank you."

Miss Draycott made the reply over her shoulder and it sounded hollow. After a moment, Rosina left her, closing the door behind her.

She waited for a moment in case she should be called back, but no sound came from behind the door, and at last she returned to her own room and sat down on the bed.

She was startled by her own storm of feeling. How she hated the man who had taken her friend's love and then so callously tossed it aside in pursuit of greed and ambition.

She paced up and down knowing that she would get no sleep that night. Sometimes she stopped and listened, but there was only silence.

At last she could stand it no longer and slipped out into the corridor. At the bottom of the stairs she found a side door, unlocked it and went out into the night.

By going round the side of the building she would be able to see Miss Draycott's balcony.

She moved out across the lawn and into the shadow of the trees. Then she stopped suddenly, alerted by what she had seen.

Miss Draycott was now standing by the open window. After a moment she stepped out onto her balcony.

She was looking up into the sky, lost in a dream and seemed completely unaware of the world around her. As Rosina watched her, she raised her arms high as though appealing to the moon and simply let herself fall.

Time seemed to stop.

Almost in slow motion she drifted down to earth while a long, mournful cry came from her. Frozen with horror, Rosina saw her fall two floors to crash onto the stones below.

Now she forced her limbs to move, racing forwards across the lawn, praying that she might be in time to save Miss Draycott, even though she knew it was useless.

She reached the figure lying on the hard stone and dropped down beside her.

Blood was pouring from a wound in Miss Draycott's head.

As if she sensed Rosina, she opened her eyes.

"I'm – sorry," she whispered. "I could not – face life – without him."

"Oh, dear God!" Rosina wept.

"But no harm must come – to him. You promise? No harm."

It took all her strength to mumble,

"I promise. I promise."

"I trust you – my dear friend."

She closed her eyes.

"*No!*" sobbed Rosina. "Not like this."

From somewhere in the distance she could now hear shouts. People had heard the cry and were running to see what had happened.

"Miss Draycott – *please* – don't go."

But Miss Draycott did not move and Rosina knew that she would never move again.

As if a spotlight had suddenly come on, Rosina saw the letter clutched in the dead woman's hand. It was *his* letter, the one that had sent her to her death. If the world saw it there would be a scandal. Everyone would know that she had committed suicide and why.

Moving too fast for thought she seized the letter. Miss Draycott's dead grip on it was tight, as though even now she was unwilling to give up her last contact with him, but at last Rosina wrestled it from her.

She just managed to conceal it in her sleeve, before Miss Baxter arrived with several other mistresses behind her.

"Great Heavens! What has happened?" she cried.

"There has been a terrible accident," Rosina told her calmly. It was strange how calm she could be now that she had made her decision.

"Miss Draycott fell from her balcony. Someone should send for a doctor."

Nobody seemed to find it strange that she should be giving orders. At that moment there was a natural authority about her and Miss Baxter immediately did as she suggested.

Rosina looked down at her night-dress now stained with blood.

"I'll go and get changed," she murmured.

She sped away before anyone could ask her questions.

Upstairs she hurried to Miss Draycott's room and went straight to the drawer in her dressing-table where she had kept Arthur Woodward's letters.

There they still were, wrapped up in blue ribbon. And there were the few trifling little gifts he had given her, and which she had treasured so much. Rosina seized them all.

There was one last thing to do. Beside the bed she found Miss Draycott's purse where she had kept her beloved Arthur's picture. Going through it swiftly, Rosina found the picture and removed it.

At the door she stopped and looked back at the room where she had known so many happy times.

"I have done my best for you," she whispered.

There was the noise of someone approaching. Quickly Rosina closed the door and returned to her own room. There she hid everything in her wardrobe, until she could find a better place. Nobody would be allowed to find those pathetic remnants of her friend's life. Her reputation would remain intact.

'It's the last thing I can do for her,' she told herself fervently. 'She also asked me to protect his reputation. I wonder if I will be able to force myself to do that.'

But the next moment she admonished herself,

'Of course I can do it. I promised her. I said that I was her friend and that's what I will be. Whatever it takes.'

She changed out of her night dress into the plainest day clothes she possessed. Then she drew her hair back severely against her head and tied it in place.

The person who looked back at her from the mirror was a stranger to her – no longer a school girl but a bitter angry woman driven by grim determination.

From the window she looked down at the stones below. A doctor had arrived and Miss Draycott's body was being lifted and carried away.

Taking a deep breath, Rosina left her room and walked downstairs to where the Headmistress was now standing distraught.

"The doctor has just pronounced Miss Draycott dead," she wept.

"I know," Rosina said. "She was dead before I left her."

"Ah yes, you were the first to reach her, weren't you? But how?"

"I was taking a little fresh air in the garden. I saw everything."

"You saw her fall?" enquired Miss Baxter eagerly. "It was an accident, wasn't it?"

"Yes, it was an accident," replied Rosina quietly. "She cried out and tried to save herself, but was unable to do so."

"Thank Heavens!" declared Miss Baxter fervently. "I mean that it was an accident. A scandal would be so terrible for the school."

"And for poor Miss Draycott," Rosina reminded her coldly. "Think of her reputation."

"She is dead and cannot be harmed now. People would never forget a scandal, but, with luck, they will forget Miss Draycott."

She hurried away, full of agitation, leaving Rosina standing alone.

'I will not forget her', she resolved. '*Ever*. And I will avenge her. I don't know how, but I swear I will.'

A noise outside drew her to the window just in time to see a rider galloping out of the school grounds. She threw herself onto her bed and lay listening.

Presently there were footsteps outside and the door of Miss Draycott's room was opening. Somebody was going inside to look for clues to the tragedy.

'But you won't find any,' thought Rosina exultantly. 'At least I have protected her that much.'

But she knew that was all she could do for the poor heart-broken woman.

As that realisation swept over her, Rosina buried her face in the pillow and sobbed for her friend who was now beyond grief or joy or help.

*

Next morning Rosina was summoned to Miss Baxter's office.

Before she went downstairs, she tried the door to what had been Miss Draycott's room. As she had expected, it was locked.

"I wanted you to know that I sent a letter by hand to your parents last night," Miss Baxter told her, "saying that after your upsetting experience you would prefer to return home."

"But my parents are in London."

"So I understand, but I received a message to say that somebody will call to collect you this morning."

'You can't wait to be rid of me,' thought Rosina. 'I've seen too much and it makes you uncomfortable. But then I never want to see this place again.'

Aloud she said,

"I will see to my packing."

A maid came to help her, and between the two of them they finished everything by the time a closed carriage came into view. Rosina wondered who had come for her.

The carriage drew up and she watched as the door opened and a man stepped out.

Then she drew in her breath sharply.

It was Sir John.

Memories of their last meeting came flooding back to her. She had told him a part of Miss Draycott's story. How hard and unsympathetic he had been.

He was the last man on earth that she would have chosen to see at this moment.

But when she went down a few minutes later, she was careful not to show her feelings.

"Good morning," he greeted her gravely. "Miss Baxter has told me what happened last night and I agree with her that this is an unhappy place for you to remain."

"What does my father say?" asked Rosina.

"He is in London. I happened to be staying overnight at your home to study some of his papers, and collect his mail. I was there when the messenger arrived and he told me what had happened. I am leaving for London today and I thought you would like to come with me and rejoin your parents."

"Thank you. I should like that."

As she returned to her room for her hat and coat, her boxes were already being taken away. Before leaving she tried Miss Draycott's door again. This time it opened.

As she had half expected, the room had been stripped of all sign of life. The sheets had gone from the bed, the wardrobe doors were open, showing emptiness inside. All sign of Miss Draycott had been swept away.

"She might never have existed," said Rosina bitterly.

"Yes, it's shocking," came Sir John's voice behind her. She turned quickly.

"I came up to see if I could be of any help."

"It's too late to help," she said bleakly. "I tried, but I wasn't really any use to her."

"Maybe nobody could have been," he suggested

27

gently.

She turned on him.

"We'll never know now, will we?"

"No, I suppose not. If you're ready, we might go now."

There was a strained farewell between herself and Miss Baxter. Then she and Sir John were in the carriage and it was rumbling away.

For a while nobody spoke and then he said,

"So Miss Draycott has died – the teacher you told me about?"

"Yes," she answered in a low fierce voice. "And she's dead because of *him*."

"I understood from the Headmistress that it was an accident. She said that you confirmed it."

"I said what Miss Draycott wanted me to say, but the truth is that she took her own life. I saw her do it."

"Dear God!"

"She killed herself because of the man you dared to defend."

"The man I – ?"

"You told me how sensibly he was behaving and how foolish she was to believe in him."

"I was not defending him, I was trying to avert a tragedy by putting her on her guard. Sadly I was too late, but honestly, my dear girl, her hopes were unrealistic."

"Of course they were," she agreed with a bright hard smile. "It is always unrealistic to place too much faith in a man."

"What exactly happened?" he asked, refusing to be provoked.

"He wrote to her saying that everything was over

between them because he was planning a wealthy marriage. He demanded the return of his letters and he wouldn't tell her the name of his bride. He made it insultingly plain that he thought she might cause trouble. Well, she won't cause any trouble now – will she?"

Her voice trembled on the last words and she buried her face in her hands, a prey to violent sobs.

"Rosina," he said, putting his arms about her and drawing her close. "Poor girl, you've had a terrible time."

"Not me," she sobbed. "She had a terrible time and now she's dead because of him. And when she lay dying, all she could think of was that he should come to no harm. Not a thought for herself, only for him. Oh, I am going to make him pay for it."

"Rosina, who is this man?"

She pulled away sharply and stared into his face, her eyes glittering.

"Do you think I would tell you?"

"I wish you would. If you're thinking of embarking on some plan of private revenge, let me beg you not to."

"To be sure, he is a fellow politician and you naturally stick together. Doubtless you would like to warn him. But you shall not, because I will tell you nothing."

"For your own sake, I implore you – "

She lifted her chin and regarded him coolly.

"I don't think we should discuss this any further, Sir John. I expect we'll reach my home soon."

He drew back, somewhat alarmed by this aloof young woman.

"I should have explained," he said. "We are not going to your home, but directly to the railway station to catch the train to London. I took the liberty of telling one of the maids to pack all your things and your trunks are travelling with us."

She knew a pang of dismay. She would have liked to go home first and find a secure hiding place for the letters she had removed from Miss Draycott's room.

But on second thoughts, perhaps it would be best to keep them with her.

Then her spirits lifted at the thought of London with Mama and Papa and the excitement of an election. So much would be happening, and there might be a little relief for her heavy heart.

CHAPTER THREE

For the rest of the journey they avoided painful topics and stayed with the safer subject of politics.

"When exactly will the election be?" asked Rosina.

"Probably not for a few months."

"A few months? As long as that? Surely, if Parliament has been dissolved – "

"It hasn't been. Even after he was defeated, Prime Minister Disraeli is still clinging on because there's a very important bill for Parliamentary reform going through. It extends the vote to men who could not vote before and it breaks up some of the larger constituencies into smaller ones."

"Change the constituencies?" she echoed, alarmed. "Yours and Papa's?"

"As you know, he has East Gradley and I have West Gradley. Now there will be a new constituency, South Gradley, formed from a part of his and a part of mine.

"But there's no danger to us. The area is solid for our party, so we'll get back in, and whoever they nominate for South Gradley will have a nice safe seat.

"The point is that both parties want this bill to succeed, so they won't dissolve Parliament until it's gone through. Then the election will be fought under the new rules."

"How annoying to have to wait."

"Be patient, little hothead. It'll happen by autumn. Your father is quite content with the delay, since it gives us time to plan instead of having to crowd everything into three weeks, as we do with most elections."

There was a slightly awkward silence before he added,

"Since our constituencies lie side by side and we do much of our planning together, your father has very kindly invited me to stay with your family until the election is over. I hope you have no objection?"

At one time Rosina would have been thrilled at the thought of seeing him every day. Now he just seemed like one of the enemy, to be judged almost as harshly as the man who had killed her friend.

But the decision was not hers and so she responded politely,

"I would never question my father's arrangements. I am quite certain that he has made a wise choice."

Sir John sighed.

"Oh dear! I predict a chilly summer."

She did not reply and a few minutes later the train pulled into London. After that the business of securing a cab made further discussion unnecessary.

An hour later they drew up outside a large house in the elegant part of London, called Belgravia, where the Clarendons lived.

When Rosina's parents had first overcome their astonishment they were delighted to see her. Sir John explained only that she had witnessed a distressing accident at school and had been sent home to recover. Then he courteously left the family alone and went up to his room.

In the library a maid served tea and cakes, which Rosina devoured hungrily.

"Sir John is staying with us for a while, my dear," explained her father.

"Yes Papa, he has already told me."

"That will please you, I dare say," he added roguishly, for he was a kindly man and an observant one.

But now he was forced to realise that the child he knew had vanished. In her place was a dignified young woman who regarded him with cool amazement.

"Indeed, Papa? Why should you think so?"

"Well, I know you've always liked him."

"I hope I have always been polite to him."

"Oh, come now, don't tell me you haven't noticed that he is a very good-looking young man," Sir Elroy countered in a rallying voice.

"I consider his looks of no interest whatever."

Faced with this queenly, offended creature, he began to realise that he had committed a *faux pas*, although he was still not quite certain how.

"Well – I was only saying – that when a young lady – that is – "

He stumbled into an embarrassed silence.

Rosina seized his hands.

"Dearest Papa, let me beg you never to speak in such a way again. If Sir John should get to know of it my position would be intolerable."

"And it would be quite inappropriate," her mother added. "I am sure Sir John is an excellent young man and all very well in his way, but – "

Her frown indicated that where her daughter was concerned, she had much larger ambitions. At the same time she gave Rosina a tiny shake of the head, indicating that she would deal with Papa.

Sir Elroy, having been put in his place by both his womenfolk, subsided into meek silence.

When they had all drunk a cup of tea and eaten some scones, the matter was past and he felt he might be permitted to speak again.

"The next few months are going to be very exciting and I'll be very glad to have you at home when we start campaigning in earnest."

"Sir John has already explained that the vote will be delayed until the autumn, because of the Reform Bill," said Rosina.

"That's right. So many more men will have the vote that the canvassing will have to be rethought. John has devised a plan of action that will be most demanding. This is going to be a most vital election and for the next few months there will be no time to think about anything else."

"Indeed there will," his wife came in indignantly. "Rosina will have her coming out ball and that is every bit as important as who runs the country."

Sir Elroy begged his wife's pardon and promised not to forget again. But he had an ally in Rosina, who was eagerly anticipating the coming contest.

"Do you really think we're going to win, Papa?"

By *we* she meant the Liberal party, of which her father was a prominent member and on whose behalf he held his seat in Parliament.

But she also meant her mother and herself. Politics was definitely a family matter.

As long as she could remember she had breathed the air of politics and had heard it discussed at every meal. At the age when other girls were still playing with dolls she knew who was in, who was out, who was 'the coming man', who had offended whom, whose bill would pass, whose bill did not stand a chance.

"We are sure to win, my dear. I have had several very interesting meetings with Mr. Gladstone – "

"Oh, dear Uncle William! How is he?"

"Eager to get on with the job. And between you and me, there have been certain suggestions – "

He stopped and seemed to become unaccountably shy.

"You'll be a Minister in the new Government?" asked Rosina eagerly.

He put his finger to his lips.

"Let us not count our chickens before they're hatched, my dear."

"But Papa, just how many chickens are there in this particular hen run?"

His eyes twinkled, but he would say no more.

*

For the next few days Rosina simply enjoyed being at home. She went shopping with Mama and bought herself an elegant inlaid box with a dainty key that secured it firmly.

"I had one like that," said Lady Clarendon wistfully. "I used it to keep letters from my admirers."

"But then, of course, when you married Papa, you destroyed them?" Rosina enquired.

"There's an excellent hat shop over there," said her Mama hastily. "Let us visit it."

Rosina would also use her box for love letters, but they were Miss Draycott's. Everything she had taken from her friend's room went in, including Arthur Woodward's picture and a lock of his hair.

Having locked it, she hid it away at the bottom of her wardrobe.

There it would stay until she was ready to use the contents to ruin Arthur Woodward.

The only thing that marred Rosina's pleasure in being home was the absence of her brother, Charles. He was seven years her senior, a handsome, strapping fellow with such a cheerful disposition and a love of outdoor life.

He had rejected with horror his father's plans for him to study law, choosing instead to enter the Navy. Having mastered his disappointment, Sir Elroy was now extremely proud of his son, who had merited fast promotion and was now a Lieutenant.

At present he was somewhere on the high seas and they were all hoping against hope that he could return home in time for his sister's ball. But it did not seem likely.

Despite the gap in their ages he and Rosina had always been very close. He was a good listener and never became bored when she confided her childish hopes and fears.

If he had been here she knew she could have told him about Miss Draycott. Now there was only Sir John and she no longer felt that she could talk to him, although he was living under the same roof.

Gradually she realised that at least Sir John had the decency not to annoy her with his presence. He seldom appeared at breakfast, was gone during the day and was frequently absent in the evening.

"He is a rising star in the party," Sir Elroy told her. "Everyone knows he is headed for high office one day and all the young ladies are setting their caps at him. Some fellows in my Club are even offering odds on which filly will romp home with the prize."

"Really, my dear!" exclaimed his wife, scandalised. "There is no need to be vulgar."

"Nothing vulgar about it," her spouse now protested. "Everyone knows that when a young man has brains and looks and is clearly headed for success, then he can take his pick."

"Well, I agree with Mama that it's vulgar," commented Rosina stiffly. "Sir John isn't a poor man. He surely doesn't need to marry for advantage. It's a disgraceful idea."

Her father stared.

"Disgraceful? Surely, my dear, now you are being unnecessarily hard on him?"

"Nobody seems to care about love any more," retorted Rosina passionately. "But I say it's the most important thing of all."

"Of course it is," replied Mama placidly. "But worldly advantage has to be thought of as well. As you say, Sir John isn't poor, but political life is very expensive."

She seemed suddenly struck by an idea.

"I know who would be ideal for him. Lettice Holden. Her father is enormously rich. Of course it's a pity he is only a tradesman. But I suppose you cannot have everything."

"He is one of the wealthiest manufacturers in the country," added Sir Elroy.

"And just what is a manufacturer but a glorified tradesman?" demanded his wife. "Mind you, with all that money he could afford to buy a title. Then he could sit in the House of Lords and enter political life that way."

"You are right," he said, much struck. "It could be an excellent marriage for John."

"We must do all we can to promote it," insisted Lady Clarendon.

Rosina regarded them, aghast. How could her parents talk like this, as though only money and influence counted?

When her father had left them she said,

"Mama, I can hardly believe what I have heard. Some people must marry for love. Surely you and Papa did?"

"Oh, yes, my dear, but if I had not possessed a large fortune, we might never have met in the first place. He was

37

a brilliant young lawyer, but not well off and needed an heiress, there is no denying that."

"*Mama*! How terrible! How could you be sure that he loved you?"

Lady Clarendon's eyes twinkled.

"Because, my love, there were two other girls whose wealth was far greater than mine and who would have been glad to have him. And he passed them over because he fell in love with *me*."

Rosina sighed to think that that was what counted as a love match.

"But I must confess to another reason for wishing to promote John's chances with Miss Holden," her mother continued. "Your father has a sentimental idea that you and John – well, never mind. I am sure you are too sensible."

Rosina drew a deep breath and looked away, conscious that she was blushing slightly.

"Far too sensible, Mama," she agreed. "I hope you can persuade Papa to abandon any such idea."

"You may rely on me. With your beauty and your accomplishments, you may look as high as you please."

"Meaning that I should marry for worldly advantage, Mama?"

"Certainly not." Her mother sounded shocked. "I hope you will marry for love."

But then her manner relaxed and the twinkle was in her eyes again as she said,

"Of course, we never know where love is going to strike, do we? Let us hope that in your case it strikes where there is wealth and position. And let's also do all we can to guide its aim."

"And how are we going to do that, Mama?"

"With lots and lots of new clothes," replied Lady

Clarendon happily.

For a while they lived in a blissful dream of visits to dressmakers and milliners. Now that Rosina was no longer a schoolgirl almost all of her clothes had to be replaced by attire suitable to an elegant young lady.

Her mother bought dress after dress. Huge, bell-shaped crinolines had disappeared to be replaced by skirts that were flatter in front, draped over bustles at the rear.

There were petticoats, chemises, bloomers, all made of silk and trimmed with satin ribbon and lace. There were dainty little hats to set atop her fair hair. There were shoes and fans.

The whole of her new attire was stylish and modern and it transformed her into an elegant Society lady virtually overnight.

She understood exactly what her mother was about. Lady Clarendon wanted a great match for her daughter, and was not prepared to see her wasted on Sir John, a mere Knight. The fact that Sir Elroy was also a mere Knight only added to her determination. Her spouse's unaccountable preference for Sir John as a son-in-law was merely one shoal to be navigated.

*

One morning, when Rosina had been home for about a week, she came downstairs dressed for riding in a new habit of blue velvet that emphasised her tiny waist and womanly shape. White lace ruffles gleamed and frothed at her throat and on her head a matching blue hat worn over one eye was the cheekiest thing imaginable.

Sir John was working in the library when she entered and his eyebrows rose in admiration.

"Perfect," he applauded. "You will break hearts wherever you go."

"That is an extremely vulgar comment," she told him lightly. "My only aim is to enjoy my ride. I do not seek to break hearts, nor would I be interested."

"Nonsense, all women want to break hearts," he responded in the same cheerful tone. "What is a man's heart for, if not for first attaching and then grinding to dust beneath an elegant heel?"

Rosina gave him a steady gaze.

"You forget, Sir John, that I have seen too much of the reality of a broken heart to find it a subject for levity. I would never want to do to any man what was done to my friend. Not that *any* man's heart could be broken to that extent."

He became serious at once.

"I'm sorry. It wasn't my intention to laugh at your friend. I had forgotten about her."

"I cannot forget. I hate the whole circus of the marriage market."

"Indeed? And yet you are becoming part of it." There was a touch of mockery in his tone.

"How dare you say that!"

"It's true. You are being groomed for the highest bidder. Intelligent as you are, you must have known that."

Her eyes glinted at him.

"And why not?" she demanded. "It seems to be something that men do every day. And, as you know, I believe in the equality of the sexes. Who says I may not do the same?"

"Not me," he said quietly. "Of course, you were always bound to be a Society lady. Now let me tell you something that will amuse you. Your Mama actually fancies that I am a threat to her plans. She as good as warned me off."

Rosina found herself blushing.

"I'm sorry," she said. "Mama should not have done that. I assured her that – "

She stopped in some confusion.

"Assured her what?" he asked, regarding her with a smile that made her feel awkward.

"That you and I had no thought of each other, nor ever would have. We have known each other too long, almost like brother and sister."

"And I've known you as a scrubby little schoolgirl," he agreed affably. "That kind of impression tends to last. I don't think I could ever quite see you as a great lady, not even when you become a Duchess. I would always remember the time you waded into that pond to rescue a cat and came out covered in weeds!"

"You would have to remember that incident, wouldn't you?" she said crossly. "Anyway, it had nothing to do with being a schoolgirl. I would do it now if there was a cat to be rescued."

"Yes, you would," he affirmed in a suddenly warm tone. "You always had a kind heart. But we are agreed in this, that I am no threat to your mother's plans."

"I wish you would stop talking in that way," she said. "You make my mother sound just like the worst kind of conniving Mama."

"I don't mean to do her an injustice, but she would not like to see us talking together like this. See, she's coming now."

Through the open door Lady Clarendon could be seen heading for the library. Rosina made a quick decision.

"Mama, I'm just going out for a ride and I am trying to prevail on Sir John to accompany me. He spends too long poring over papers and needs the exercise."

"I am sure that your Papa – "

"Papa is away today. He will not object. But Sir John is unaccountably trying to refuse, which I consider most ungentlemanly. Do order him to say yes."

"My dear, your manner leaves much to be desired. It is a question of propriety – "

"But he's practically my brother and I can quarrel with him far more enjoyably than anyone else."

Outmanoeuvred, Lady Clarendon was forced to yield.

"If Sir John can spare the time, it would be very kind."

"I am, of course, at Miss Clarendon's service," he declared, his eyes dancing. "It will take me but a moment to change."

When he had departed Lady Clarendon said,

"I don't know what you're thinking of, Rosina."

"Merely to show you that your fears are groundless, Mama. While I am still not 'out' he is an acceptable escort and why should I not make use of him?"

She finished with a shrug that was a masterpiece of indifference. Lady Clarendon seemed reassured by this common-sense view and made no further problems, beyond reminding her daughter not to be too late returning.

Left to herself in the library, Rosina tapped her riding whip against one elegantly shod foot and felt pleased with the way she had fired the first shot.

At one time, when she had been girlishly infatuated with Sir John, she would have been glad to know that her father favoured him. But that now seemed a long time ago, before he revealed himself as one of the heartless throng who condemned poor Miss Draycott to death.

Now they were opponents even if he had not yet realised it.

Just the same when Sir John reappeared in riding garb,

she had to admit that he looked splendid. He was smiling too in a teasing manner that, for the moment, she found acceptable.

"What a clever creature you are at getting your own way," he said, "and what a devil of a life you will lead some poor fellow. Remind me never to propose marriage to you."

"Remind me to refuse if you do," she countered.

He joined in her laughter and they left the house in perfect accord.

As they cantered towards Hyde Park she remarked,

"I hope I didn't drag you away from anything really important."

"Nothing that cannot be done this afternoon. It's most helpful to me to have the use of your father's library."

"Are you making plans for the future?" she asked.

"We're all doing that in one way or another," he replied enigmatically.

As they turned into Hyde Park he asked,

"How is your plan for revenge going? Have you taken any action yet?"

"I am biding my time," she replied austerely. "So far that man's path hasn't crossed mine."

"And I hope it never does."

He saw the wry look on her face and hurried to add,

"And that isn't because I want to protect him, but because I want to protect you."

"Then you're worried about the wrong person," she told him. "My part in this affair is the avenging angel."

"I can see you as an angel, but not flaming with vengeance."

"That is because you do not know me."

When he did not answer she turned her head and saw

him peering into the distance. Following his gaze she saw two young women seated on horseback. One of them was waving.

"You know those ladies?" asked Rosina.

"The one waving is Miss Lettice Holden and the lady sitting next to her is Lady Doreen Blakemore."

He waved back and they began to canter forward, followed by a groom who remained at a discreet distance as the young people met.

Rosina studied Miss Holden with interest. So this was the bride her mother had chosen for Sir John.

There was no doubt at all about her wealth. It was proclaimed by the thoroughbred horse she rode and the fashionable riding habit she wore. On one shoulder she sported a glittering diamond brooch. It was clearly valuable, but at this hour of the day and on this garment it was out of place and the effect was slightly vulgar.

Her companion was far more discreetly and elegantly dressed. She was the daughter of an Earl, but it was her air of breeding that announced this to the world.

Sir John introduced the ladies to each other and Lady Doreen immediately clasped Rosina's hand.

"I am so glad to meet you," she began. "I've heard such a lot about you."

"About me?"

"Papa is very interested in politics and he admires Sir Elroy greatly. I know that they have dined together several times at the House."

By 'the House' she meant the Palace of Westminster by the Thames, home to the House of Commons and the House of Lords. She too had breathed in a political atmosphere all her life and she used the term as casually as Rosina herself would have done. It was an immediate bond between them.

As the four of them began to ride together, Rosina and Lady Doreen fell naturally into conversation, while Miss Holden joined Sir John just behind them.

Rosina could hear them laughing and concluded that Sir John was well pleased with his company.

For herself she found Lady Doreen to be charming. So far her closest friendships had been at school, but now school was behind her and she must learn to be at ease in the social world.

Lady Doreen had made her debut earlier that year and was full of eager advice when she learned that Rosina had yet to 'come out'.

"You will find your life transformed," she told her. "Balls, parties, lovely clothes." She added in a low, confiding voice. "And young men. Of course I shouldn't say that. Dear Mama would be shocked. Even after her debut, a girl is supposed to cast down her eyes while the men study her critically."

"But why shouldn't *we* study them critically?" Rosina wanted to know.

"That's what I say. We have our opinions too and it is not just a matter for Papa to decide – whatever he may think," she added darkly.

"Is your Papa trying to make you marry someone you don't care for?" Rosina asked, shocked.

"Not exactly. He has introduced me to several men that he approves of and I always know that he's hoping I will choose one of them. But he is too kind to force me.

"He recently encouraged a young man who was very dull but worthy and he made it plain that he wanted me to accept him. But I simply could not and I said so to Papa. He was most displeased, so I will have to wait for his annoyance to blow over before I can tell him that – well – "

She stopped and coloured.

"There is someone else?" suggested Rosina delicately.

Lady Doreen nodded, her blush becoming even more pronounced.

"He has not actually – that is, we have not – there are difficulties and his delicacy prevents him from speaking. But we each know how the other feels."

"I hope all goes well with you," said Rosina warmly. "For I most fervently believe that love is the only thing that matters – far more than wealth or advancement."

"Oh, so do I," agreed Lady Doreen fervently. "How wonderful that you understand! I feel that we are going to be the greatest of friends."

"I think we should be going now," Sir John called from behind them. "We shan't be forgiven if we're late for lunch."

"Nor shall we," Lady Doreen laughed.

They all exchanged farewells. As they were turning away, Miss Holden called out roguishly,

"I am usually riding in Hyde Park at about this time."

"I shall look out for you," Sir John assured her.

"Make sure you do," she told him. "I count on you."

Rosina decided that she did not like Lettice Holden.

CHAPTER FOUR

It was wonderful how Lady Clarendon's manner to Sir John thawed when she learned of this encounter.

On her return back home Rosina told her everything, including how much in sympathy she and Lady Doreen seemed to be, although she left out some of the details of their conversation as unsuitable for a mother's ears.

"So you think John is much taken with Miss Holden?" she asked eagerly.

"He certainly seemed happy to ride beside her for some time," said Rosina.

"Excellent. It will be a splendid match. You and he must ride together often and doubtless you will meet her again."

"We certainly shall. She as good as informed him so in a manner I thought rather forward."

"It may have seemed so to you, my dear, but depend upon it, he had given her reason to feel confident. You and he must go out often."

"I thought you were afraid he was going to sweep me off my feet," observed Rosina, not entirely pleased with the way this conversation was going.

"Oh, that's all in the past. He's going to marry Miss Holden. We must do what we can to expedite matters."

But before she could take any action, there was a development.

*

Rosina came downstairs the next day to find her mother talking to Sir John, obviously excited over something that had just arrived in the mail.

"An invitation Mama?" she enquired smiling. "But we have many invitations. What is so exciting about this one?"

"It's from Lord Blakemore," exclaimed her mother. "He is giving a dinner party and we are all invited. You must have made a great impression on his daughter yesterday and this is the happy result. I have always hoped that we could get to know him better. He is such an important man in the House of Lords and he could help your father so much."

"Then we must certainly get to know him better," agreed Rosina. "Nothing is more important than Papa winning his seat, the Liberals winning the election and Uncle William giving Papa a Ministry."

"Oh, darling, you sound more like a politician every day."

"In this family I could hardly help it," answered Rosina gaily.

"I know, my dear, but it sounds slightly alarming in a young girl. You should be thinking of your debut, planning a guest list."

"But I am, Mama. We must make sure the list includes everyone who can be useful to Papa."

She made this remark with an impish look that made her mother laugh, but she was also half serious.

"And afterwards we must see about finding a husband for you."

"Mama!" she protested with a chuckle, "there is no

need to say that as though I was some plain Jane, past her last hope."

"I don't believe anyone could think that," said Sir John wryly.

"Take no notice of her, John," her mother smiled. "She is only fishing for compliments."

"Well you just won't have any trouble finding me a husband if Papa is made a Government Minister," Rosina said ironically. "The men will flock around me."

"My love, you are so cynical."

"But it's true. There is no better dowry for a girl than a powerful father. Isn't that so, Sir John?"

She gave him a challenging look, reminding him that he alone knew what she was really talking about.

"I am the wrong person to ask," he said lightly. "I've never been on the catch for a husband."

Lady Clarendon gave a little scream at this witticism.

"What a wicked thing to say! I just hope you will tell Rosina that she really must never speak so frankly in company."

"Oh, but we're not in company now, Mama. I say what I like in front of Sir John."

"But perhaps you should *not*," parried her mother wide-eyed.

"Why not? We are old friends and I am not on the catch for him, so it doesn't matter if I shock him."

"Ignore her, ma'am," Sir John said grinning. "She is trying to terrify us, but don't give her the satisfaction of succeeding."

"She just terrifies me all the time," admitted Lady Clarendon with an alarmed glance at her daughter.

The dinner party was only three days away, so clearly they had been invited as an afterthought. Rosina supposed that her mother was right and her meeting with Lady Doreen was in some way connected.

This suspicion was reinforced by the discovery that Sir John had also received a last minute invitation. Doubtless Miss Holden would also be present.

It was Rosina's first really important dinner party. Since she was not yet officially 'out' she was not, strictly speaking, supposed to be invited to join such exalted company. But it was normal for a *debutante* to attend a few events prior to her ball, so that she could become used to Society.

Her dress was a vision of tulle and satin in a delicate shade of pink. How different she already looked from the schoolgirl she had been recently, she thought. Now she could show off her tiny waist and elegant bosom.

But there was more than her grown-up figure to mark the change in her. Her eyes held a sad angry knowledge, which should not have been there.

'Here we all go, waltzing off to the marriage market,' she thought. 'Mama has set her sights high for me, because she doesn't think Sir John is good enough for me – not that I would want him anyway. And he is pursuing an heiress. I thought better of him, but *et tu Brute*!

'And the Blakemores, of course, want Lady Doreen to marry a man of higher rank than herself. But she at least gives love its proper place and will hold out against them. I must do my best to support her.'

Then she sighed and murmured,

"Poor Miss Draycott! What chance did you have in this grasping world?"

*

She and her parents travelled to Blakemore House together. Sir John was delayed by a meeting and would be following later.

As the carriage rumbled through the London streets Lady Clarendon commented,

"I am so glad that you struck up a friendship with Lord Blakemore's daughter."

"Nobody could help being her friend," said Rosina. "She is delightful."

"How fortunate! And even if she were not, it would still be advisable for you to seek her friendship."

"*Mama*!" exclaimed Rosina, half laughing, half protesting. "I do wish you would stop scheming for five minutes."

"When you're a mother, scheming is necessary," insisted Lady Clarendon, unperturbed. "You will find that out one day."

The carriage had stopped.

Looking out, Rosina saw that Blakemore House was magnificent. She knew its reputation as one of the finest residences in all of London.

The Earl was a great man and his patronage could be very useful. This was the first time that Sir Elroy and his family had been invited. Although wealthy, they were not of great social importance. But now that he might become a Minister, his value was enhanced.

As they entered through the grand front door with stone lions sitting on each side of it, Rosina's eyes widened at what she could see. There was no doubt that these palatial surroundings were very agreeable.

The butler admitted them and led them down a large passage with magnificent pictures on the walls.

Then he opened the door and announced in a stentorian voice,

"Sir Elroy and Lady Clarendon, and Miss Rosina

Clarendon, my Lord."

Following her father and mother into the drawing room, Rosina thought it was one of the most attractive and magnificent rooms she had ever seen.

There were several windows looking out on to the garden. There were so many flowers which not only made the room look lovely, but also scented it.

The Earl greeted them. He was a man in late middle age with a large head of grey hair and an imposing manner.

"Good to see you, Clarendon," he said heartily. "My love, allow me to introduce – "

As they all exchanged the proper pleasantries, Rosina began to look around her and saw that their hostess was glittering with diamonds and bracelets.

She began to feel that both she and her mother were somewhat inadequately dressed. Each of them wore a necklace and a brooch in contrast to the Countess who seemed to be smothered with jewels.

Rosina's father was a prosperous man and although his fortunes had originally been founded on his wife's dowry, he had risen in his profession and now earned large fees as a lawyer.

But now Rosina began to realise that the Blakemore's wealth was on another level entirely.

Then before anything else was said, the door opened and Lady Doreen came hurrying in. She was petite and exquisitely dressed in a fashionable gown of pale blue silk. Her fair hair was arranged in a way which made it seem almost like a coronet and her jewels were clearly worth a fortune.

"And here is my daughter, who always manages to be late," said the Earl in a fond voice.

"I am sorry, Papa, but I was riding and forgot the

time," apologised the charming young woman.

"My daughter rides better than any man," the Earl boasted. "And she can forget everything in favour of a horse."

"Mine is the same," added Sir Elroy, drawing Rosina forward. "But I understand that you two young ladies have already met on horseback."

"Indeed we have," agreed Lady Doreen, embracing Rosina. "I am so glad to see you again. We are already such good friends."

"But of course," agreed the Countess. "You will always have so much to talk about. Horse lovers can talk their heads off, sometimes until dawn is breaking."

They all laughed and Lady Doreen drew Rosina aside.

"Wasn't it clever of me to arrange this? Now we can see each other often. I knew from the first that we were deeply in sympathy and it will be like having a sister to confide in."

"What about Miss Holden?" Rosina could not resist asking. "Can you not confide in her?"

Her companion made a face.

"I like her very well, but we see things differently. She is more impressed by great titles than I am and she would regard my wish to marry a poor honest man as madness."

Something impelled Rosina to say,

"But she is interested in Sir John, who does not have a great title."

"But he is exceedingly good looking," Lady Doreen teased.

"I disagree. I think his looks are no more than ordinary."

"Well, I can tell you that Miss Holden thinks he is extraordinarily handsome."

"Then Miss Holden is welcome to him," retorted Rosina. "But she should be aware that he is a mere Knight, as my Mama would say."

Lady Doreen's eyes twinkled with mischief.

"Oh, ho! Your Mama is afraid that you will make a match with him."

"I – don't know what you mean," said Rosina, confounded.

"She is trying to put you off him. She plans something more exalted for you. But what are *your* wishes? A woman should have her own ideas at all times, otherwise she is in a poor position to counter her parents' schemes."

"I agree," said Rosina firmly.

"So do tell me, my dear friend. What are your plans? Oh, forgive me, I was forgetting. You are not 'out'. You have yet to look around you."

"That is true, my debut will be in a few weeks."

"And then all the young men will flock around you and you can make your own choice. We will strike Sir John off the list – "

"He was never *on* my list," insisted Rosina.

"Well, we'll strike him off anyway and yield him to Miss Holden."

"That will suit me admirably," declared Rosina stiffly.

"Will he be here tonight? I know he was invited, but I don't see him."

"He has a meeting to attend, but I believe he said he would come on afterwards," answered Rosina in a voice that clearly indicated that it was nothing to her whether he was at this party or not.

The room was becoming crowded. Lettice Holden arrived with her parents. All of them were dressed in ways that puffed out their extravagant wealth. Lettice, in particular, dripped with diamonds in a way that was quite unsuitable for a young girl.

A young man appeared beside them. Although not handsome he had a kind face and a merry grin which inspired Rosina's instant liking. Lady Doreen introduced him as her eldest brother, George. He regarded Rosina with evident admiration, while his sister beamed on them both.

When George had moved away to greet other guests, Rosina asked Lady Doreen,

"And the gentleman you have been telling me about? Will he not be here?"

"Oh, yes, he has been acting as Papa's secretary and now he's been nominated to fight one of the new seats at the election. He's been invited because Papa regards him as a man of great talent, who should be encouraged."

"But not where *you* are concerned, it seems."

Lady Doreen gave her impish chuckle.

"I can do all my own encouraging. Oh, Rosina, I love him so much. Not that I tell him that, of course. I leave him in doubt so that he isn't too sure of me, but I long for the day when we can proclaim our love openly."

She stopped suddenly with a little gasp and her hands flew to her mouth.

"There he is! Oh, look at him. Isn't he wonderful?"

Smiling, Rosina turned to look at the doorway, where a young man, splendid in evening dress, had just appeared.

Then her smile faded.

She stared in horror, hoping to discover that this was no more than a bad dream.

The man was *Arthur Woodward*.

It was impossible, she told herself wildly. It simply could not be true.

But it *was* true. This was the man she had seen in the

teashop that day, making eyes at the woman who worshipped him to the point of idolatry and whom he would soon betray.

Now another woman worshipped him, unaware that his cruelty had killed Miss Draycott.

He looked fine, thought Rosina bitterly, standing there in the doorway, apparently diffident, but actually allowing time for all eyes to fix admiringly on him.

He was handsome, elegant, perfectly groomed. Also he had an air of authority and an obvious pride in himself that made him appear to be very much at home in this glittering company.

Only she knew that he was a cruel, heartless schemer.

She watched as Lord Blakemore summoned him to be introduced to someone of note and saw his ingratiating manner.

And she hated him.

Finally, when he had oiled his way around the assembled company, he came over to where the girl who loved him was waiting.

"Forgive me," he said contritely to Lady Doreen. "For myself, I longed to come to you at once – "

"But you had your duty to do first. Arthur, let me introduce my friend, Miss Rosina Clarendon. Rosina, this is Arthur Woodward."

He bowed low over her hand and she had to fight not to snatch it away in disgust.

"Miss Clarendon, this is an honour. I admire your father greatly. In fact, everyone who knows him must admire him."

She longed, as she had never longed for anything before, to reply by telling him how much she hated and despised him. But that was impossible, so she murmured conventional thanks.

There was something in his eyes, as they met hers, which made her shiver. Clearly he was assessing her and she could tell that he thought she was rather attractive.

He smiled at her in a way which made her want to strike him.

"I suppose you realise that I shall be standing for South Gradley, the new constituency next to Sir Elroy's," he stated, speaking as though the whole world must now be interested in him.

He smiled at her as he continued,

"It is not as large as his, but I'm hoping, almost against hope, that I will, with a great deal of help from Lady Doreen, win the seat."

"I imagine it must be very challenging to be the first in a new constituency," remarked Rosina. "And of course you are most fortunate to have the power and influence of the Blakemores on your side."

She could not keep a slight bitter emphasis out of her voice, but he did not notice. Nor did she expect him to. This man was blinded by vanity and assumed that everyone took him at his own estimate.

"I am indeed fortunate to have Lady Doreen on my side," he replied smoothly. "She has promised to canvass for me, and I know she will do it brilliantly."

He smiled at Lady Doreen.

"Are you listening?" he asked. "I am singing your praises."

"So I should hope," she said at once. "Otherwise I will go and work for the opposition."

"You are wonderful!" purred Arthur, looking at her as he spoke.

As their eyes met, Rosina knew exactly what Lady Doreen was feeling. It was the same as Miss Draycott had felt just before she received that fatal letter and it was terrible to witness.

She turned away biting her lower lip to prevent herself from telling this man what she thought of him.

Lady Blakemore bustled up to them.

"I hope you two aren't talking politics again. I declare, Miss Clarendon, my girl is always trying to engage Mr. Woodward in political discussions, when I am sure he gets enough of them with my husband."

Lady Doreen smothered a giggle, and Rosina knew that whatever their discussions were about, it was *not* politics.

"Sir John Crosby," announced the butler.

Sir John entered the room quietly and was warmly welcomed by the Blakemores. When he had done his duty he made his way to the little group in the corner, smiling at Rosina, bowing low over Lady Doreen's hand and then doing the same for Miss Holden, who simpered and sighed.

It seemed that he had met Mr. Woodward on a previous occasion and they exchanged bows.

Suddenly a silence fell over the room. Everyone looked up to see a new arrival standing in the doorway. He was in his late fifties with a strong face, a beaky nose and sharp penetrating eyes. At his side was a plump comfortable looking woman.

"Mr. and Mrs. William Gladstone," announced the butler.

Lady Blakemore hurried to greet the great man who led the Liberal party and who was widely expected to be the next Prime Minister. The room began to buzz again.

Arthur Woodward's attention was riveted.

It took the Gladstones some time to greet everyone, because so many people wanted some of the great man's time. When he came to the Clarendons, he shook hands and stood talking intently with them in a way that everyone agreed was very significant.

Then his eyes warmed as he saw Rosina.

"And now how is my dear god-daughter?" he asked, hugging her.

"All the better for seeing you, dear Uncle William," she exclaimed, embracing him and then embracing Mrs. Gladstone, who also greeted her warmly.

Lady Doreen had met Mr. Gladstone before, but she was not his god-daughter. There was an extra warmth in his greeting of Rosina and she sensed that Arthur Woodward was aware of every nuance as his sharp eyes darted from one to the other.

It was time to go in to dinner and Rosina found herself sitting between two gentlemen whom she did not know, but with whom she fell easily into conversation.

On the other side of the table she could see Lettice Holden flirting shamelessly with Sir John.

But her efforts would be useless, Rosina felt sure. He had far too much delicacy to be attracted to such a vulgar young woman.

She also had a good view of Arthur Woodward who was sitting beside Mrs. Gladstone, turning all his charm on her and neglecting the sad looking spinster on his other side.

Afterwards the ladies retired to have coffee in the drawing room, while the gentlemen stayed over their port.

When they finally joined the ladies, Arthur came straight over to Lady Doreen.

Now he had many secret things to confide which only she could hear.

'I hate him,' Rosina muttered again to herself. 'I hate him and I will never, never in the whole of my life fall in love with a man like that. All he cares about is what benefit she can bring him.'

As she thought of the loving letters he had written to Miss Draycott, she wanted to get up and hit him over the head, then to tell the whole world how corrupt and appalling he was.

But she could not do so in this house. Her father needed Lord Blakemore's friendship.

'But only his friendship,' she thought angrily. 'Papa always pays his own election expenses, while Mr. Woodward will be having *his* paid by the Blakemore family.'

At that moment the young man looked up and caught Rosina's eye. Smiling, he came to join her.

"May I fetch you some more coffee?" he asked.

"Thank you, I should like that," she said as warmly as she could manage.

She had decided that it was time she became better acquainted with Mr. Woodward.

And, of course, he wished to become better acquainted with the daughter of a man who might soon be in a position of power.

"I haven't had the pleasure of meeting you before," he began, returning with the coffee.

"I'm not really 'out' yet," she explained. "In fact, I was only recently at school."

"I find it hard to picture you as still a schoolgirl," he said. "You seem so confident and sophisticated."

"You're too kind. In my last year at Laine Hall, we were taught how to behave in Society."

There was a perceptible rattle from the cup in his hand, she was glad to note.

"Did – you say – Laine Hall?"

"That's right. It's a school on the edge of Papa's

constituency. Have you heard of it?"

"I – believe so."

"Have you been to that part of the world recently?"

"I – yes – that is," he stammered. "It's near my own constituency – the one I hope will be mine – "

His face turned pale.

"Then, of course, you pay frequent visits," persisted Rosina smiling implacably, "to make yourself familiar with the place."

"That is – one of my duties."

"I should really have been at school now, but I had to leave early owing to a very upsetting experience."

"I am sorry to hear that." He had recovered some of his smooth manner.

"Well, the experience was not mine, but that of a good friend of mine, a teacher called Miss Draycott."

He neither moved nor spoke, but his face was the colour of death.

"Perhaps you have met her, Mr. Woodward?"

"*No,*" he said, the word exploding from his mouth like a bullet from a gun. "Why should you think I – that is – I don't believe I've had that pleasure."

'I could almost believe you,' she thought, 'if I hadn't seen you sitting with her in a teashop, holding her hand and gazing into her eyes.'

"No," he said again, "I never met this lady, but I do recall hearing of her – that she left the school without warning. Friends who wrote to her were informed that she had departed suddenly."

'Of course,' she mused. 'After I left, you grew nervous because she didn't return the items you had asked for. I expect you wrote, reminding her, but your letter came back with a note to say that Miss Draycott had left without leaving an address. Since then you have been on hot coals wondering where she is and what she did with your compromising letters.'

"Yes," she said aloud. "She did depart very suddenly indeed."

"Do you happen to know where she has gone?" he asked with an attempt to sound casual.

Rosina drew a deep breath and looked him straight in the eye.

"*She is dead*, Mr. Woodward."

It did her good to see the look that passed across his face.

It was one of stark terror.

CHAPTER FIVE

Rosina spent the rest of the evening in a mood of angry excitement. She had struck a blow for Miss Draycott and it was a thrilling experience.

Now that she had seen Arthur Woodward at close quarters, she hated him even more than ever. His ease of manner, his assurance, only made her think of her friend lying dead.

Fairly soon after their encounter she went to her father's side and said, so that only he could hear,

"I think we ought to go home. You have a great deal to do tomorrow and if you are tired you will find it very difficult."

He smiled at her.

"You are quite right," he agreed. "We must go home. But I have enjoyed coming here tonight and I hope the Earl's daughter will stay your friend."

He lowered his voice.

"I hear they have parties almost every week. That is just what you would enjoy, I am quite certain."

"Actually I enjoy being with *you*," replied Rosina. "I believe we will find it difficult to concentrate on anything else until the election is over!"

Her father laughed.

"You are quite right, my darling, but I think you have had rather a difficult and unhappy time recently and now I want you to enjoy yourself. So if the Blakemores ask you to come again, you must accept."

Before they left, Arthur Woodward sought her out.

After their brief conversation, she had turned away, giving him no time to reply and she could tell that he had been agitated ever since.

He uttered the conventional words of farewell, but his anxious eyes seemed to bore into her, as if, in that way, he could seek out her true meaning.

It was with difficulty that she shook him by the hand.

"It has been a great pleasure to meet you and your parents," he said to her. "I wish for your father the same success that I long to have myself."

He paused for a moment.

Rosina knew that he expected her to give him words of encouragement and flattery.

Instead without speaking she walked away. She could sense him staring after her, wondering why his charm did not seem to work. Or perhaps fearful that the reason was the one he suspected.

"Is Sir John not accompanying us?" she asked when she and her parents were in the carriage.

"I saw him deep in conversation with the Holdens," replied Lady Clarendon. "No doubt they will convey him in their carriage."

So the Holdens were determined to sink their claws into him, Rosina thought. On the other hand, it was a relief, as she wanted to speak about Mr. Woodward without alerting Sir John.

"Do you think that Mr. Woodward is likely to win in South Gradley?" she asked her father innocently.

"I think he is going to have a tough time," responded her father. "A new constituency is always difficult. Don't tell me he took your fancy. I thought your manner to him was rather cool when we said goodbye."

"He most certainly did not take my fancy. I have no wish to meet him again."

"Perfectly right, my love," chipped in her mother.

Rosina was tired and retired to bed as soon as they reached home. But she did not, as she had expected, fall asleep at once.

She lay awake until nearly two o'clock, when she heard the sound of a carriage in the street below. Climbing out of bed, she went to the window and looked down to where Sir John was just entering the front door.

Strangely enough, after that it was even harder to go to sleep.

*

The following morning Rosina and her mother settled down to the serious business of planning her debut ball.

The guest list was glittering, since Papa knew not only the Blakemores, but almost all the great titles in the House of Lords.

"The Duke of Allion will be coming with his eldest son whose engagement has just been broken off," said Lady Clarendon with satisfaction.

"Mama, that is going much too far," retorted Rosina, laughing. "You can't marry me to a Duke, not unless I had as much money as the Holdens."

"Ah yes, the Holdens. They must be invited for John's sake. You do well to remind me."

"I didn't mean – "

"And the Blakemores will bring their eldest son whom you have already met – "

Rosina gave up, convinced that her mother was beyond reason.

"Now Miss Kennington will be here this afternoon to discuss your dress and then – yes, Amesbury?"

"Mr. Woodward has called, your Ladyship," the butler informed her.

"Indeed?" Lady Clarendon did not look pleased at this visit by a penniless man. "Very well, show him in please, Amesbury."

"Surely you cannot have encouraged him?" she asked Rosina when the butler had gone.

"No, Mama. He doesn't please me at all. But he is so obviously seeking to ingratiate himself in Society that I suspect he is calling on everybody."

"Let us hope it is no more than that."

He entered apparently all at ease, smiling, full of practised charm, uttering words of thanks to those who had been 'so kind' to him the previous evening.

But Rosina was not deceived. She saw his pallor, his dismayed glance at her mother. He was on edge, longing to find out more from herself, but unable to speak unless he could see her alone.

Lady Clarendon spoke to him politely but without warmth and she did not offer him refreshments. Rosina replied to his questions as briefly as possible.

He grew paler still as he realised that he would not be able to talk to her alone.

Then just when it seemed that he had no choice but to leave, Sir Elroy walked in and greeted the young man cordially.

"Woodward!" he exclaimed, shaking his hand. "I hear fine things about you from Lord Blakemore. Well, I expect we will be seeing you at my daughter's ball, eh? That's right. Everyone will be there."

"Thank you, sir. I shall greatly look forward to it."

Defeated, Lady Clarendon had no choice but to murmur,

"I shall send you an invitation, Mr. Woodward."

"I shall look forward to it eagerly, Lady Clarendon."

"Come and talk to me, my boy," invited Sir Elroy jovially, sweeping the visitor off to his study.

Lady Clarendon waited until they were out of earshot before saying carefully,

"I have only admiration and respect for your Papa, who is clearly going to be a great statesman. But sometimes I wish he would mind his own business!"

*

Rosina's debut dress was glorious white silk, adorned with tiny white rosebuds. The skirt swept back to a bustle that swished elegantly as she walked and the bosom was cut lower than any dress she had ever worn.

With it she would wear her mother's dazzling pearl jewellery, taken out of the bank where it was normally stored and now cleaned and reset. As well as a necklace there was a tiara, ear-rings and bracelets.

The guest list swelled every day. The Blakemores were coming, so were several other titled families, including several from the opposite political persuasion to the Clarendons. Sir Elroy was a popular man in both Houses of Parliament and, as he said,

"This is a party, not a political convention. I shall invite all my friends, no matter what they believe."

"There is a rumour that Mr. Disraeli himself will be coming," Sir John told Rosina.

"I can hardly believe it."

"Mr. Disraeli likes a good party and this is rapidly becoming *the* party to attend. Anybody who was excluded could never hold up their head again. You are going to be the belle of London."

"But, of course," she said carelessly. "Look at who my father is."

"No," Sir John corrected her quietly. "Not because of him. Because of yourself. I know that some men will chase you for gain. That's the way of the world. But most of them will admire you for your honesty and sweet nature."

There was a note in his voice that she had never heard before. It disturbed her obscurely and she quickly riposted,

"You are very uncomplimentary, sir. You don't say they will admire my beauty."

"I thought we could take that for granted," he smiled.

"Then you are mistaken," she teased him. "Women do not like having their beauty taken for granted. They prefer it to be mentioned."

"Some women do like to have their looks praised constantly," he agreed. "But I don't think you are one of them. You have a good mind and a generous heart and you should never marry until you find a man who values them above looks, above advancement and above money."

There was something in his tone that touched her heart and for a moment she almost softened. But the mention of money conjured up Lettice Holden and inwardly she drew back.

"Then I think I shall never marry," she came back with a careless shrug, "since where is such a man to be found? Nowhere, I would have thought."

"Don't," he said fiercely. "Don't talk like that."

"I shall speak as I please. How dare you try to give me orders!"

"I do not order. I implore. You are about to enter a world where everything is for sale and all true values are turned upside down."

"Do you think you have to tell me that?" she flashed. "Haven't I reason to know it?"

"Yes, that is what makes me afraid for you. You are so full of anger and mistrust, but I beg you not to become hard and suspicious."

"No, I should be stupid and trusting like other girls and believe everything a man tells me."

"Of course not. It is right that you should remember your friend, but don't let it turn you against the world. You are sweet and gentle and that is just what makes you lovable, not – "

He checked himself abruptly.

In his eagerness he had seized her hands and was holding them tightly. There was a burning light in his eyes as he looked at her, and she could feel his warm breath fanning her face.

Startled, Rosina gazed back at him so that their eyes met and she seemed to be looking directly into his soul. At the same time she had a disconcerting feeling that he too was looking into her soul.

She took fright. How dare he do this, as though every thought and feeling she had was opened up to him. How dare he understand her!

She snatched her hands back, turning away from him.

"Forgive me," he said. "I didn't mean to – what you do is none of my business."

"Indeed it is not," she said in a shaking voice.

"I wish you every success Miss Clarendon. You deserve the best that the world has to offer."

Without warning she found herself on the verge of

tears. She took a moment to control herself, then turned back to smile at him, wanting to be friends again.

But he had gone.

*

At last the night of Rosina's debut ball arrived. The great ballroom was gloriously decorated with flowers, the orchestra was taking its place, beginning to tune up.

Rosina stood in front of the mirror, taking in the sight of herself in her fabulous white dress. Pearls gleamed softly in her hair, in her ears and around her neck.

She drew a long breath, trying to believe that this vision was really her.

"My love, you look so beautiful!" gushed her mother ecstatically. "All the men will fall in love with you."

"I don't want to be greedy, Mama," said Rosina demurely. "Five or six will do!"

Sir Elroy appeared and kissed his daughter.

"You look lovely, my dear."

"Oh, Papa, if only Charles had managed to be here!"

"I know. His last letter said that he would do his best, but obviously it wasn't possible. Now we must go down to greet our guests, who will be arriving soon."

The three of them walked out into the corridor just as Sir John appeared from his room. He stopped and stood looking at her as if he could not believe his eyes.

"Miss Clarendon," he stammered, "may I say that you look – *magnificent*?"

"Thank you kind sir. And you too look exactly *right*."

He was in white tie and tails and looked, she was sure, more splendid than any man had ever looked.

"Thank you, ma'am," he bowed slightly.

She pulled herself together. It would never do to let

him think she was gaping at him.

"I am sure Miss Holden will approve," she muttered, recovering herself.

"Miss Holden?" echoed Sir Elroy, who was not quite abreast of events. "Is she – ?"

"Don't let us stand here chattering," his wife broke in with a determined smile. "Our guests await."

The four of them walked down the broad staircase just as the butler opened the door and announced the first arrival.

In a short time the ballroom was filled with all the most glittering names in London, whether political or aristocratic, or both.

To Rosina, 'Uncle William' was the greatest man in the room, since she was sure William Gladstone would be Prime Minister in a few weeks.

But Mr. Disraeli was still the Prime Minister and to have drawn him to their house was a coup. He was in his sixties and splendidly ugly. Beside him was his wife, twelve years his senior and with an excited manner that concealed a shrewd brain.

Like everyone else Rosina was charmed by them and their devotion to each other. At the same time, she could not help viewing 'Dizzy' slightly askance.

"Everyone knows he originally married her for her money," she murmured to Sir John.

"True, but I have heard him say so openly, joking, and then announce that he'd do it again for love. However it started, it is a love match now."

He added wryly,

"Besides, aren't you trying to marry me off to a rich wife?"

She gasped at this frankness, but before she could reply, he said,

"Ah, I see her now. Excuse me."

Infuriated she watched him walk over to the Holdens, and raise Lettice's hand to his lips.

At that moment there was a small commotion by the door. Rosina turned her head just as her mother gave a little shriek of joy. The next moment they were both racing across the floor to greet the newcomer.

"Charles, my dear boy!" Lady Clarendon cried, hurling herself into her son's arms. "You managed to get here."

"I have only managed just a few days' leave, but I wouldn't miss Rosina's ball for anything," he replied.

He kissed his mother, clapped his father on the shoulder and then embraced his sister.

"You look wonderful, sis," he told her affectionately.

"So do you," she said sincerely, for Charles was in the full dress uniform of a Naval lieutenant and it suited his tall handsome figure.

There was a flurry of introductions. Everyone wanted to meet him and everyone was impressed by his handsome, laughing countenance, especially the ladies.

After that the evening went by in a whirl of success. Mr. Disraeli himself begged the first dance with Rosina, then Uncle William. If Rosina had wanted to flaunt her high political connections, she was being given every chance to do so.

The young men competed for her hand. She danced with the heirs of Dukes, Marquises and Earls. Twice she danced with Lady Doreen's brother, George, the pleasant young man whom she had met at their house.

As they twirled around the floor, she studied the other dancers and saw Sir John with Miss Holden and Lady Doreen dancing with Arthur Woodward.

As they passed each other he looked up and their eyes met. There was the same look of fear that she had seen before and she was not surprised when he approached her as soon as the dance was over.

"May I have the honour of this next dance, Miss Clarendon?" he asked.

"Very well," she agreed, rising and giving him her hand.

She danced in silence, refusing to make things easy for him.

As last he said desperately,

"I was most interested in what you were telling me about Laine Hall, Miss Clarendon."

"Do you mean the death of my friend, Miss Draycott?"

"I – yes. I was most distressed to hear about it."

"Really? Did you know her then?"

He blenched.

"I was not personally acquainted with her – "

"Really? That's not what your letters say?"

This time he almost stumbled.

"I really don't know what you are talking about."

"'*I know that you will understand the need for me to do this*'," she said, quoting from his last fatal letter. "I feel sure you recognise those words."

"I – I – " he swallowed convulsively.

"Or how about these? '*I beg you to return my letters. They can have no meaning for you now*'."

Rosina's eyes flashed.

"No meaning, Mr. Woodward? What passed between you may have had no meaning for you, but she loved you with all her heart and she died for it."

"But surely – her death was an accident?"

"That is what the world believes because I have protected her reputation by removing all trace of *you*."

For a moment his face showed his relief, but the next moment she snatched it back from him again, saying,

"You will never get those letters back, Mr. Woodward, or your picture, or the gifts you gave her, or the lock of your hair."

"Oh, Heavens! Miss Clarendon – "

"I trust I make myself clear."

He began to burble.

"You don't understand. I meant no harm. It was a wild infatuation but she misunderstood. She thought I meant more than I did."

"Don't force me to quote your own words to you again."

"I meant no harm," he repeated. "It was just a misunderstanding. I have my way to make in the world, and I'm ambitious, which surely is not a crime? You think badly of me, but I know I have it in me to be a great man and be of service to this country, if only I can make a start."

He was talking very fast, almost falling over his words in an attempt to make her see matters his way. Rosina listened with contempt.

"And you intend to 'make a start' with my friend, Lady Doreen?" she asked sweetly. "I don't think that is a very good idea."

Suddenly his face became hard and cruel.

"Miss Clarendon, if you are planning to thwart me, let me advise you against it. I have made my plans and I will not be deterred now."

"Are you threatening me?" she asked lightly. "How very foolish of you. I am not Miss Draycott, all alone in the world."

He realised he had erred and backtracked hastily.

"You misunderstand me – I only meant to say that my intentions are good and the country will benefit if I am allowed to serve as I mean to and – and – Miss Clarendon, I will do anything if only you will return my letters."

"But I will not return them."

"*You must*," he insisted frantically.

In his agitation he raised his voice, causing several heads to turn in their direction.

"The dance is ending," said Rosina. "It has been such a pleasure talking to you, Mr. Woodward."

"But – "

"Miss Clarendon," came a welcome voice.

It was Sir John, appearing by her side, ignoring Arthur Woodward.

"I believe the next dance is mine," he said, opening his arms.

"So it is," she said, swinging into them and whirling away from Arthur, who was left glowering.

"Why was Woodward becoming so agitated?" he asked. "What is it that you must do – marry him?"

"*Certainly not.*"

"Then what were you talking about?"

"That does not concern you," she countered loftily. "Suppose I asked you what you talk about with Miss Holden?"

"Chiefly about her father's money."

"What?"

"She introduces the topic in every conversation. I think I must know what every one of her diamonds is worth, plus all the other jewels that she could have worn but didn't."

"How vulgar!"

"But you are the one who pushed me into her arms," he said innocently. "And I must say, I am very grateful to you."

She glowered at him but he continued, unperturbed,

"After all, a man has his way to make and in that respect Mr. Woodward is an example to us all."

"What do you mean?"

"Look at him."

Following his gaze she saw what he meant. Arthur Woodward was talking to the Prime Minister, his head inclined at an intent angle as though he lived only to drink in the great man's words.

"But Mr. Disraeli is a Conservative," protested Rosina. "We are trying to drive him out of power."

"Obviously Mr. Woodward is protecting himself from both sides," commented Sir John blandly.

"You don't mean that he – surely not?"

"Why not? His position is precarious. The party has not even nominated him for South Gradley yet. And if they do, who is to say he'll win it? It's a new constituency and could go either way. I cannot make myself like Woodward. I think he'll do anything, even making up to you because of your father. Don't listen to him."

"He's not making up to me."

"Are you sure?"

"Quite sure?"

He gave her a strange look and then asked quietly,

"Is it *him*?"

"What do you mean?"

"Is *he* the man Miss Draycott loved? He is, isn't he?"

She shrugged.

"And you were threatening him?" he exclaimed quite

astounded. "Good grief! I have never heard anything like it. Don't you know what a dangerous thing you're doing?"

"Why should it be dangerous? There's nothing he can do to me." Her eyes kindled. "But there's a great deal I can do to him."

"Rosina, I beg you, give up this idea."

"I won't give it up. You didn't see my friend fall, as I did. I held her in my arms as she was dying and I'll never forget it. Nor will I ever forgive him. I hate him and I always will."

"Rosina – " he pleaded. "Rosina – please."

Something in his voice seemed to go through her, making her tremble. He spoke her name with a soft yearning note that was unbearably sweet to hear. She wondered if he used that same tone to Miss Holden.

"Don't," she said. "Don't say any more."

"You are right. Talking is dangerous. Dancing is better."

He was right, she thought. Who cared for words when she was in the arms of such a superb dancer?

Fleet-footed, he now swept her across the floor and suddenly she felt a sensation of soaring, as though her body had been created to move in time with his.

If only, she thought as she spun round and round in his arms, this wonderful feeling could go on forever.

But when the dance was over she wondered at herself. This was only Sir John, whom she had decided was an enemy.

But sometimes it was hard to remember that.

CHAPTER SIX

The next morning the door knocker never stopped. Bouquets and gifts arrived for Rosina every few minutes, plus a stream of invitations.

"You are the belle of the Season," her mother now proclaimed in delight.

Rosina and Charles went riding together in Hyde Park.

Lady Doreen and her brother appeared and the two couples fell in together. Charles edged his way forward so that he could ride beside Lady Doreen, while Rosina fell back and chatted to George, who was in a downcast mood.

"Debts," he mourned. "They just pile up."

"You mean you're extravagant?" she teased.

"And I gamble a bit," he confessed. "Well, more than a bit. Papa is furious, but he doesn't know everything."

"More gambling debts?"

He looked uncomfortable.

"And a few other things."

"There's nothing for it," Rosina now quipped merrily. "You will have to marry an heiress."

"You are quite right," he sighed. "I would ask you, since like all the others I'm madly in love with you. But I don't think you have nearly as much as I need."

At this Rosina laughed so loudly that the other two

turned to look at her and Lady Doreen observed to Charles how well Rosina seemed to getting on with her brother.

"I dare to hope that she has a partiality for him," she said.

In a sense she was right. Rosina did have a partiality for poor George, but only a sisterly one. She especially appreciated the honest way he had confessed his situation, thus clearing the air between them of any misunderstanding.

After that they were the best of friends and he confided in her problems he did not dare to tell even to his sister.

They met repeatedly at parties and balls, glittering, colourful occasions that she realised made up the marriage market. She despised it because of Miss Draycott, but she also found some of the Season very enjoyable.

She often met Arthur Woodward at social gatherings. He was popular and known as a man with a promising future, and there were several houses, with daughters, where he was made welcome.

In Rosina's presence he was always careful to conduct himself with decorum, but he never ceased trying to talk to her alone. Sometimes she avoided him, sometimes she permitted him a word or two.

Sir John was often present at these parties and she was always conscious of his eyes on her whenever Arthur came near.

At one evening function, where the guests were being entertained in the garden under trees hung with coloured lamps, she found Arthur Woodward by her side.

"I must talk with you," he muttered.

"I have nothing to say to you, Mr. Woodward."

"But I have much to say to you, madam. I will not tolerate having a sword hanging over my head."

"And I will not tolerate you buying your way into

Society by making false love to innocent women. Keep your distance from young ladies and behave like a gentleman."

She could see that he was inwardly seething with rage, but caution forced him to keep his voice low.

"You have property of mine that I want returned," he growled through gritted teeth.

"I have nothing that belongs to you."

"My letters – "

"Letters belong to the recipient, who was dear Miss Draycott, and she entrusted them to me. You might call me her *executor*."

Driven beyond endurance, he seized her wrist and dragged her into the darkness beneath the trees.

"Don't play games with me," he snapped.

"I am not playing," she assured him. "If you are so sure these letters belong to you why not make a legal challenge and we'll face each other in court?"

Even in the dim light she could see him grow paler. She knew he couldn't risk anything that might expose the contents of those letters.

"Leave my friend alone," she told him, "or I'll ruin you."

"It's not as easy as you think. I have made – certain pledges – to Lady Doreen, and if I was to – that is – "

"If you were to offend her now, she might complain to her father who would withdraw his influence," supplied Rosina. "You will simply have to take that chance, because I will not allow a man like you to marry her. Now let me go."

She wrenched herself free of him and ran away back into the light almost into the arms of Sir John.

"Good Heavens, what's happened?" he demanded.

As he spoke he took hold of her and she felt how much

more pleasant it was to be held by Sir John than to be held by Arthur Woodward.

"Take me home," she begged. "Just take me home, please."

He did so, putting his arm about her and hurrying away towards the waiting carriage.

Neither of them saw Lady Doreen standing there alone watching Rosina's departure with a face full of disillusion.

*

The following morning Rosina was alone when the butler announced,

"Lady Doreen Blakemore, madam."

The girl who entered the room was unlike the person Rosina knew. Gone was her youthful exuberance. Now her face was sad and haunted.

"How could you do it, Rosina?" she asked with tears in her eyes. "I thought we were friends. I trusted you and you try to take my Arthur from me."

"I? – try to take him from you?" she echoed astounded.

"I saw you last night, running out of the trees and Arthur coming out after you. You had been together. Don't try to deny it."

"I don't, but – "

"I spoke to him and he confessed everything."

"He did?"

"He told me how you had tried to come between us because you wanted him for yourself."

"*How dare he!*" Rosina exploded. "Me? Want that greedy, deceitful, callous, heartless, lying – *me*?"

Despite her distress Lady Doreen now stared at her, astonished and impressed by Rosina's forcefulness.

"It's true that I have tried to break you up and I won't

give up until I've done so. But not because I want him myself. He is the last man I could ever want."

"Then I just don't understand you," questioned Lady Doreen.

"Mr. Woodward is not the injured innocent he pretends to be. Only very recently he was writing passionate love letters to someone else, swearing eternal fidelity, saying that no other woman in the world could mean anything to him.

"She fell madly in love with him and every day she waited for him to propose. Instead he wrote to her breaking it off, saying he had found a better match. The poor woman was devastated."

Lady Doreen had recovered her composure and was looking at Rosina with scorn.

"And this woman – I suppose she is *yourself*?"

"Oh, no," Rosina said sadly. "Her name was Elizabeth Draycott, and she was my friend."

Lady Doreen stared at her.

"Was?" she asked.

"Yes, was. She is now dead."

The other girl made one last attempt.

"I do not believe you. This is all lies."

Rosina sighed.

"In that case, come upstairs. There is something I must show you."

Reluctantly Lady Doreen followed her up to her room and sat down as far away from Rosina as possible.

Rosina pulled out the box where she kept the letters, unlocked it and took out the contents.

"Here are all the letters he wrote to her," she said, handing them over.

Her friend read in silence for some minutes before

saying bleakly,

"This is his handwriting and these are the self-same phrases he has used to me. And this – "

She was holding the final letter, the one that had driven Miss Draycott to her death.

"This one is dated a week after he and I met, when he was already speaking words of love to me. He was already planning to marry me for mercenary reasons, wasn't he?"

"I am afraid he was," said Rosina gently.

"I don't understand. How do you come to have these?"

"As I have told you Miss Draycott is now dead. She threw herself off a balcony and died in my arms. I took these letters from her room to preserve her reputation.

"In her dying moments she thought only of him. She wanted no harm to come to him, so I tried not to injure him. I simply told him to leave you alone, under threat of being exposed. But I would never have exposed him, if he had simply backed away from you.

"But when he told you such lies about me, I had no choice but to defend myself with these letters."

"She is dead," murmured Lady Doreen. "She died for love of him. How terrible."

"Bad news is always terrible," said Rosina. "Forgive me for the distress this must cause you, but believe me, if you had married him you would have been wretched."

"I would give anything not to believe you, but I cannot ignore these letters."

"I promise you that every word I have told you is true," answered Rosina. "I don't want you to be caught and tied to such a despicable man. He is selfish and dangerous."

"You were right to tell me," agreed Lady Doreen, "but it has been a shock. I thought, I suppose stupidly, that what he was saying to me he had never said to any other woman. That I was the one woman he had been looking for."

She fell silent, sunk in sadness.

Rosina regarded her with sympathy.

At last she said,

"I am afraid that is part of his act and he does it very well. But I'm certain that poor Miss Draycott was not the first person he had made love to, nor will she be the last."

"What am I to do?" Lady Doreen pleaded. "I had promised to help him canvass in his constituency, if he was adopted as candidate. I cannot do so now, but Papa will wonder why. Perhaps I could tell him that I've promised to help you canvass votes for your father, as we are such good friends."

She looked quickly at Rosina.

"We are friends, aren't we?"

"Always," Rosina replied fervently. "Forgive me if this has hurt you, but it would have been worse for you to learn the truth later."

"You are quite right," murmured Lady Doreen in a soft voice.

"Don't allow yourself to be sad for long," Rosina told her impulsively. "He isn't worth it, and what you have learned from him may be useful in dealing with other men. You have so much to offer that the wrong sort of man will always imagine you are easy prey."

"Then he will find himself mistaken," asserted her friend in a resolute voice. "I will wait for the right man."

"I am so glad you said that," added Rosina. "He must love you because you are the perfect woman he has been looking for and perhaps praying for all his life. As you are so pretty and very intelligent, I think that, sooner than you expect, you will find the right person who you will love and who will love you for the rest of your life."

She paused for a moment.

"That is what we all want. Of course I want it too, but – " she broke off and sighed. "I don't know if it will happen for me."

"But all the men are sighing for you," said Lady Doreen.

"But I am not sighing for them."

"And I thought you wanted to take Arthur away from me."

"I did – but only to toss him on the rubbish heap where he belongs," Rosina replied with spirit.

At this Lady Doreen even managed a faint laugh.

"I should thank you for being brave enough to take action against him. "I would never have suspected and I believed Arthur when he told me I was the first woman who had ever captured his heart."

There was a sob in her voice as she continued,

"Now I see that all he cares about is personal gain."

"Unfortunately that is true," admitted Rosina. "But not all men are like him, and sooner or later we will each find a man who loves us because we are ourselves, and not because we have anything else to offer him."

"But how shall we know?" Lady Doreen wondered. "How can girls like ourselves ever be sure ?"

"I think we know instinctively. You will see love in his eyes and know that love is beating in his heart. It's not what he says that matters, but what he is thinking and feeling. That is what we have to be clever enough to understand."

Lady Doreen said sadly,

"Suppose we never find a man who loves us for ourselves."

"You need not fear that. You are so pretty and so charming that you will find a man who would love you if you owned nothing but a hole in the hedge."

"But if it doesn't happen," Lady Doreen persisted.

"Then we'll be happy old maids."

They embraced, hugging each other tightly.

"We shall always be friends," promised Rosina.

Together they walked downstairs.

But there a shock awaited them.

As they reached the hall, the butler was opening the front door, admitting a man who stopped dead at the sight of them.

They too stopped suddenly.

"*Arthur*," whispered Lady Doreen.

One look at her face was enough to tell him the worst, but he tried to brazen it out.

"I have come to take you home," he blustered. "I hope you haven't been listening to any lies about me."

"I have been listening to the truth," Lady Doreen told him passionately. "Don't come near me. I never want to see or speak to you again."

"But I can explain – " he cried, refusing to believe that the prize was slipping through his fingers.

"Your letters? Can you explain them? I have seen them, Arthur. I have read every dreadful word and there is nothing that you can explain."

A moment ago she had been smiling through her tears, full of courage. Now the sight of him had brought her grief flooding back. Her face streaming with tears, she ran down the rest of the stairs, pushed Arthur Woodward aside and ran out into the street.

Rosina saw her run to her waiting carriage and hurry

aboard. It drove off at once, leaving him staring after it in helpless rage.

Then he turned back into the house, staring at Rosina with eyes filled with hate.

The butler looked nervously between them.

"It's all right, Amesbury," said Rosina quickly. "You may go."

Whatever was going to happen now, she did not want it witnessed and gossiped about by a servant.

The butler melted away.

"*You* did that," Arthur Woodward snapped.

"You brought it on yourself by telling lies about me," she told him. "But then, lies come naturally to you, don't they, Mr. Woodward?"

"You are determined to ruin me. You would not rest until you had taken revenge for that stupid woman."

"Don't talk about her like that."

"I shall talk any way I like. Do you think I care for anything after what you have done to me? I could have made something of myself. I could have served this country – "

"No, you only cared about serving yourself. I could not let my friend marry you, knowing what I do."

"And just what do you think will happen now, my fine lady? Am I supposed to slink away like a beaten dog because you have deigned to turn your hand against me? Do you think I give up so easily?"

"I care nothing for what you do now."

"Oh, but you will. Matters are not going to rest here. I too know how to take revenge and I shall take it. You will rue the day you ever crossed me, I promise you."

"And you will rue the day you ever spoke to a lady like that," came Sir John's voice, so suddenly that they both jumped.

He wasted no time but took Arthur Woodward's ear between his fingers and propelled him irresistibly towards the front door.

"Let me go," he howled.

"By all means," snarled Sir John, releasing him so suddenly that the man staggered and had to clutch the doorpost to stop himself falling down the steps.

"You haven't heard the last of me," he raged. "I'll make you sorry for this, both of you, but especially – " his finger pointed directly at Rosina, "especially *you*!"

Instantly Sir John sprang forward, seized him by the collar and thrust him back against the wall.

"If you dare to hurt one hair of Miss Clarendon's head," he declared with fierce emphasis, "I will make you sorry you were ever born. Do you understand me?"

Arthur Woodward gave a gasp to signify that he did and Sir John released him. He turned and ran down the steps, down the street and out of sight.

"Are you all right?" Sir John asked Rosina.

"Yes, I am very well. I won't let that creature frighten me. But I am glad you came by when you did."

"It was no accident. Amesbury was worried about leaving you with him and he came to find me, thank goodness. Are you sure that you are all right? You seem upset."

Rosina had begun to shake.

Sir John drew her quickly into the library and shut the door behind them. Then he simply drew her into his arms so that her head rested on his shoulder. Gradually she felt herself stop shaking.

"That's better," he said. "You should never have been left alone with that beast."

"Why not? I promise you he was far more afraid of

me than I of him."

"And that's where your danger lies. A man like that fights like a cornered rat and I don't want you to be his prey."

"He can fight all he likes. Lady Doreen knows the truth now. What can he fight for?"

"Revenge. You just heard him. My poor girl! You shouldn't have to carry all these burdens."

The words made her stiffen and draw back.

She was reluctant, because it was strangely pleasant to be standing like this with him. But not for the world would she let Sir John think she was the kind of frail female who demanded male protection.

That was probably how he believed women ought to be, she thought darkly. If so, she would show him otherwise.

"Why not?" she demanded. "Why shouldn't I have to carry these burdens?"

"Because carrying burdens is a man's responsibility and – "

He stopped, warned by the glitter in her eyes that he was straying into dangerous territory.

"I know you are stronger than most women, and more intelligent – "

"Oh, so you think most women are weak fools?"

"I didn't say that."

"You implied it."

"Why are you trying to quarrel with me? Are you angry because for once you needed my help?"

"I am grateful for your help, but don't read too much into it. I am still stronger than that man."

"Don't underestimate him, Rosina."

"Then let him not underestimate me. I still have the letters and, if I catch him up to any mischief again, I'll use them."

He gave a rueful laugh.

"You are so brave and defiant. If I didn't know you better, I would be scared of you myself!"

"What makes you so sure you know me better? You knew me as I used to be, not as I have been since Miss Draycott's death. I am a different person since then. I fight back – on her behalf and on behalf of all women. And I will not be satisfied until all women are empowered to fight for themselves."

"Are we talking about women having the vote?" he asked wryly.

"Amongst other things and how dare you find that funny! Do you think what happened to her is funny? Has anyone ever been able to treat you like that? I don't think so."

"Then you would be wrong," he said. "I have been treated exactly like that by a woman who broke my heart and left without a backward glance as soon as she found a better prospect. Callousness is not the prerogative of my sex, believe me."

"Then you should be much more sympathetic and understanding when I try to do something for other women."

"But you have already done it. I merely beg you not to endanger yourself. Rosina, you've struck a mighty blow for ill-used women, but let this be the end. Promise me that."

"I shall promise you nothing. How dare you demand promises of *me*!"

"I not only demand, I insist. Let me have those letters at once."

"I shall do no such thing. Who do you think you are? My father?"

"Not at all," he muttered so softly that she barely

heard.

Out loud he said,

"You are brave and strong but you don't know the world."

"I knew it well enough to defeat Arthur Woodward."

"He isn't defeated, only winded. He'll be back. And if you like to think of yourself as a warrior, let me tell you this. No warrior is invincible and only the foolish ones imagine that they are. You need help."

"I do *not* need your help."

"I think you do."

"Your idea of helping me is to take over and give me orders."

"I want you to give me those letters."

"And I think I should not. The subject is now closed."

"Is it indeed?" he asserted, his eyes kindling with anger.

"Yes, it is, because I am now going upstairs to my room, where I shall lock myself in. If you attempt to pursue me, it will cause a scandal. In fact, Mama would probably throw you out of the house."

"And your father would promptly bring me back," he retorted, annoyed with himself for being unable to resist saying it.

Rosina surveyed him with her head back. She was almost laughing.

"You delude yourself, sir. Papa may be a very big man in the House of Commons, but in the House of Clarendon, Mama rules. If you doubt me, try it."

He did not dare try it. She was too sure of herself. Instead he said through gritted teeth,

"That is dishonest fighting. It's taking advantage of

your opponent's weak spot."

"I thought that was how you were supposed to fight," she replied innocently. "Isn't that how politics works?"

"Then suppose I fight dishonestly too? Either you give me those letters or I will disclose this whole affair to your father and he will demand them."

"You wouldn't!"

"Why not? I am simply playing you at your own game. As you say, it's politics and you are becoming an accomplished politician. So we fight on even terms."

Rosina's eyes shone with excitement.

"No quarter asked?"

"None asked or given," he said.

"In that case – I have the letters upstairs."

She left the library and mounted the stairs, Sir John behind her. As they reached her room she said,

"You'll have to wait out here."

"Naturally," he readily agreed, slightly shocked at the suggestion that he might do otherwise. "But leave the door open so that I can see what you're doing."

"Why, don't you trust me?"

"No."

She slipped into her room.

The next moment the door was slammed in his face and the sound of a bolt shooting across told him he had been fooled.

"*Rosina*!"

From behind the door came her triumphant voice.

"There's more than one way to fight dishonestly."

He was about to knock furiously, when he beheld the terrible sight of the housekeeper approaching. He thought fast and raising his voice, addressed the door,

"I am glad to have been of service, Miss Clarendon."

Then he turned and walked down the stairs with as much dignity as he could muster.

And her laughter followed him all the way.

CHAPTER SEVEN

Next day Sir John went to attend to some business in his constituency and Rosina did not see him for a while. Meanwhile her giddy social life went on whirling until it was almost out of control.

As a *debutante* she was presented at Court and was winked at by the Prince of Wales. She attended parties, balls and picnics. She joined a merry group at the races where the Prince had a horse running, put a discreet wager on the animal and lost.

Miss Holden was there and lost a great deal of money, which seemed to bother her not at all. George Blakemore also had substantial losses, which he shrugged off.

For a few days she did not see Lady Doreen and she wondered what had happened regarding Arthur Woodward, who seemed to have vanished from the Social scene. She was thinking of calling on her, but then she saw her at a ball they both attended, given by the Duke of Malton.

Her friend smiled and came over to her.

"I've been hoping to see you," she began. "I have so much to tell you."

They drew aside together into a side room.

"Tell me what happened," begged Rosina. "Did you send Arthur Woodward on his way?"

"Oh, yes. When I reached home Papa was there and

he could see that I was upset. He wanted to know why and so I had to tell him everything. He was displeased that I had encouraged Mr. Woodward's pretensions, but he forgave me.

"I told him about the last letter, the one in which that man boasted of the match he was about to make and Papa was furious. He sent for him and told him never to set foot in our house again. Since then Papa has been warning people to have nothing to do with him."

"I am so glad," said Rosina fervently.

"And now Papa wants to speak to you."

Lady Doreen took Rosina's hand and led her to Lord Blakemore, who said gruffly,

"My daughter has told me what she owes you, ma'am, and I thank you. Should you ever need anything, you may command me."

"Thank you, sir. I am only glad to have been able to help my friend."

She smiled at Lady Doreen.

"And you have been the best possible friend to her," said Lord Blakemore warmly. "It was my intention to back Mr. Woodward as a candidate for the new constituency of South Gradley. But now I have withdrawn my backing. I did not, of course, say why for my daughter's sake. I simply made my lack of enthusiasm known and I am happy to say that his candidacy is at an end."

"That's wonderful news," exclaimed Rosina.

"Yes, but don't be too sure that you have seen the last of him. He has an ingratiating manner and he will find another opening in some place where my influence does not extend."

"Is there such a place?" asked Rosina.

"He will discover one. When I think I esteemed him so highly that I was going to let Doreen canvass for him, it fills me with horror."

"But perhaps she can join me in canvassing for Papa," suggested Rosina.

"That's what Doreen tells me she would like to do. It will soon be time for us all to go to the constituencies."

"And I should so like to help Sir Elroy win his seat," came in Lady Doreen eagerly.

"Of course you may, my dear. Miss Clarendon, I bid you goodnight. And please remember that you have my eternal gratitude."

Almost overwhelmed, Rosina thanked him. She could hardly believe what was happening. Arthur Woodward was defeated and she only wished that Sir John could be here to witness her victory.

In fact now any gathering from which he was absent seemed strangely lacking in interest. If he was present she could at least enjoy a good quarrel with him!

But then, she realised, even if he was here, he would probably be too busy dancing with Lettice Holden to have any thought for herself.

Miss Holden was dancing with George Blakemore, but as the music ended George hailed her and came over to ask Rosina to take the floor with him. She danced with him twice, then with several other highly placed admirers who praised her to the skies. One, a Marquis, was clearly laying the ground for a proposal until she gently discouraged him.

Finally she returned home, filled with relief to have escaped her admirers, who frankly were beginning to bore her.

As she descended from the carriage and approached the front door, something made her turn and look towards the end of the street.

She gasped.

For an instant she had almost imagined that she saw Arthur Woodward standing there glaring at her.

But the place where she had seen him was empty. She must have imagined it. Then the butler opened the front door and she went inside.

'I am beginning to imagine things,' she told herself. 'It's Sir John's fault, trying to make me afraid when there's no need. This is my night of triumph and nothing is going to spoil it. But it's a pity he is not here to see it.'

*

These days Sir Elroy was staying later and later at the House of Commons and it was clear that matters were coming to a head.

"The Reform Bill is in its final stages," he told his wife and daughter one evening. "As soon as it has passed, Parliament can be dissolved and we can really concentrate on the election."

Time seemed to drag on forever and still Sir John did not return. Rosina was surprised to realise that he had only been away for two weeks since it felt like months.

One evening she and her Mama returned home very late from an evening where she had again been the belle of the ball. Lady Clarendon was in ecstasies over her daughter's success.

"But I must just put you on your guard my love. You gave three dances to the Honourable David Conroy, who after all is only a younger son."

"But he makes me laugh, Mama."

"Ah, yes!" sighed Lady Clarendon. "Your Papa used to make me laugh when we first met. Sometimes he still does. I know how attractive it can be. But still – *a younger son.*"

"I suppose younger sons must marry somebody,"

observed Rosina.

"But there is no need for them to marry you," replied her Mama, dismayed by the turn the conversation was taking.

"I wonder when Sir John will return to London," said Rosina in a carefully indifferent voice. "With matters now moving so fast in Parliament, surely his place is here?"

"I am sure Sir John knows his own business best."

"He is also supposed to consider Papa. He ought to be here," said Rosina crossly.

"Well, I expect he will return soon."

This time Rosina said nothing, but her fingers tapped nervously on her reticule.

When they reached home Lady Clarendon went into her husband's study, while Rosina now picked up some invitations that had arrived while she was out.

She glanced up as her mother returned, saying,

"Well Sir John has returned, so I hope you'll be satisfied now."

"He's here?"

"Yes, he's in the library with your Papa. They are working very hard. I told them what a great success you'd been tonight and they said to give you their congratulations. They apologise for not saying goodnight to you, but they are so very busy."

"I wouldn't dream of disturbing either of them, Mama. Goodnight."

She kissed her mother and hurried up the stairs to her room, where she closed the door a little too sharply.

*

The following morning Rosina endured an awkward meeting with her father, who had summoned her into his study.

"My dear, whatever have you been up to now?" he enquired.

"What do you mean, Papa?"

"I have heard such disturbing stories – about Arthur Woodward and a young teacher at your school called Miss Draycott. And you knew all about him and have been – I scarcely dare to say the word – blackmailing him?"

So Sir John had told Papa all about it. At that moment Rosina felt that she hated him.

"I knew that he had behaved badly, Papa, and was behaving badly again. So I stopped him."

"Without confiding in your parents? Good grief, I never heard such – "

He stopped as the door opened and Sir John entered.

"I am sorry to disturb you," he said, "but that package has arrived."

He handed over a large envelope, which Sir Elroy seized eagerly.

"Thank you, John. Leave me now. We'll talk later."

Rosina swept out of the door, followed by Sir John, who closed it behind them.

At once she turned on him.

"I would never have thought it of you," she rasped at him bitterly.

"Thought what of me?"

"You betrayed me to Papa. You broke your word."

"Never. If you mean the letters, I gave no promise about them."

"And so you told him everything."

"I swear I did *not*. How can you think such a thing of me?"

"He knows all about it. He just said to me – oh, the same sort of things that you said."

"They are the things that any man must say when he thinks that you are in danger. Can't you understand that?"

"You told Papa," she persisted stubbornly.

"Did he say so?"

"He didn't get the chance, but when I next see him I shall ask him – "

"And have me thrown out of the house," he said wryly.

"What do you mean by that?"

"I didn't say anything about Woodward, but if you inform him that I knew, he is going to be annoyed with me for *not* telling him. I should have done so, of course. So, if you want to do me a bad turn, go ahead."

Rosina glared at him sulphurously.

At that very moment the door opened and Sir Elroy emerged. He looked askance at Rosina.

"We'll talk some more on that matter later," he said.

"Yes Papa, but will you tell me how you knew about it all?"

"Why, Lord Blakemore told me, of course. I asked why he had withdrawn his patronage of Woodward and he explained what he had discovered with your help. Why? Who else could it possibly have been?"

"Nobody Papa. I wasn't thinking. I will leave you two now, because I am sure you have much to discuss."

Rosina fled.

She was blushing all over at the injustice she had done to Sir John. How could she have been guilty of such a terrible accusation?

That afternoon a dressmaker called with the gown made of shimmering blue satin that she was to wear that night. On her feet she wore elegant silver sandals and her head was adorned with Mama's diamonds.

She knew she was a vision of beauty, but for some reason she could take no pleasure in it.

She could not be happy until she had seen Sir John and apologised.

Mama would not be attending the ball tonight, as the Blakemores were collecting her.

When Rosina heard the carriage arrive outside, she began to descend the stairs slowly.

As she came around the curve in the stairs she saw Sir John standing in the hall below. He wore white tie and tails, as though he was going to the ball.

He looked up and saw her.

Then he grew very still.

There was a look in his eyes as they rested on her that made Rosina's spirits soar. He watched as she descended and then reached out to take her hand as she took the last step onto the floor. She waited for him to speak, but he did not. He seemed transfixed by the sight of her.

At last he spoke.

"Rosina," he said softly. "Rosina – "

Her heart was beating too hard for her to speak. She wanted to say something, but no words would be enough to answer what she saw in his eyes.

The world seemed to stop.

"My dear, are you ready?"

The sound of her mother's voice broke the spell.

She came out of her dream and returned to the present. It seemed to be the same with him.

"Yes, Mama," she called, drawing back from him.

Lady Clarendon appeared in the hall in a flurry of

agitation.

"The carriage is here. Sir John will go with you, he is also invited. Enjoy yourselves, both of you."

The butler was opening the front door and Sir John offered her his arm. Rosina took it and they swept out together.

The magic moment was over.

She still had so much to say to him, but now it was impossible. Sitting in the carriage with the Blakemores, they could speak of nothing but trivialities.

But the chance would come at the ball, she thought. He would ask her to dance and they could talk then.

But he never did ask her. He danced with Lady Doreen once, with Lettice Holden twice and with every other beauty in the room, it seemed to Rosina. But he never once approached her and, in fact, left the ball early, saying that he had urgent papers to read.

To Rosina it sounded like a feeble excuse.

Later that evening the Blakemore coach dropped her at home and then carried on with Lady Doreen.

As Rosina entered the house her mother opened the door to the library, beckoning her and Rosina went in.

"Was it a good evening?" asked Mama. "Did anything happen?"

By 'anything' she meant a proposal.

"Lord Senwick made me an offer, Mama," Rosina told her listlessly.

Lady Clarendon's hands flew to her mouth.

"You are engaged to Lord Senwick?"

At that moment Rosina became aware that her father and Sir John were in the room listening.

"Oh, no, Mama. I refused him."

Lady Clarendon gave a little scream.

"You turned him down? Without consulting your father or me?"

"He's a rather stupid man. When I try to talk politics he says he wouldn't dream of burdening a lady's head with anything so dreary. Honestly, what can you say to such stuff?"

"Nothing at all," said Sir John cheerfully. "He is clearly beyond redemption."

Lady Clarendon ignored this remark.

"But you rejected him without even consulting your parents," she repeated, trying to make her stubborn daughter understand the enormity of her offence.

"But I don't want to marry him, Mama."

"What has that to do with anything?"

Rosina saw that Sir John was regarding her satirically. Against her will, her lips twitched.

"I thought it might have a little to do with it," she countered mildly.

"You know very well what I mean. He's an *Earl*."

"Well, he's a very stupid Earl."

"My dear child, you are looking at this in quite the wrong way. His brains or the lack of them are totally irrelevant."

Rosina's eyes met Sir John's and read in them a wicked humour that matched her own.

"How very fortunate for him!" she murmured.

"If we all started demanding intelligence in a man before we could marry him, what would the world come to?"

"Nothing. The human race would die out," supplied Rosina mischievously.

Her father gave a choke of laughter. Instantly his lady

turned on him.

"Have you nothing to say to your daughter, sir?"

"Yes, I would like to commend her for refusing a stupid man."

"You are as bad as she is," his lady informed him.

"Surely not, ma'am," said Sir John, sounding shocked.

Lady Clarendon dismissed this as a mere pleasantry, but Rosina knew better. Sir John, wicked creature that he was, had meant that nobody was as bad as herself. She threw him a wry look to show that she fully comprehended and he grinned back.

Of course she understood him, as he understood her.

Despite their differences, they could read each other's minds and would always be able to do so.

Even when they were old and grey, she realised, they would still share that perfect sympathy of mind that was as strong as love. So strong, in fact, that it would be there even when they were married to other people.

For some reason she felt depressed.

*

Next day she sought out Sir John.

"I want to apologise to you for the wicked things I said. I should have known you wouldn't betray me."

"Yes, I think you should have known that," he said with gentle reproach.

"I'm sorry. Are we friends again?"

She held out her hand. After a moment he shook it.

"Friends," he said.

She felt disappointed. Somehow she had expected more, but she could not have said what.

"So what exactly has happened to Arthur Woodward?" he asked. "I have heard rumours, but I haven't liked to ask questions of anyone but you. He is no longer the candidate for South Gradley. Lord Blakemore saw to that."

"How?"

"He simply withdrew his support and Woodward was finished."

"And no doubt that satisfies you?"

"It delights me."

"Rosina, do you really think that's how things should be done?"

"With a man like him, *yes*."

"But with another man? One who wasn't guilty?"

She frowned.

"What are you saying?"

"I am saying that Lord Blakemore raised his eyebrow and everyone hastened to do his bidding. And that is wrong. It doesn't seem wrong in this case because we know Woodward is a bad character, but can it be right that one man should have so much power? Especially when it is exercised behind the scenes?"

"But so much is done behind the scenes," protested Rosina. "Much of it could not be done at all otherwise. I am not sorry that it has happened. How else could he have been defeated without a scandal?"

"I understand that, but – "

"I don't think you do. You are a man and men can fight openly, but women can not."

"Of course but – "

"We have to seize on every weapon we can find, even if it's not very satisfactory. That's why I went to war against that man in the way I did, and why I would do it again. What are you smiling at?"

"I was thinking that poor Senwick has had a lucky

escape. Fancy imagining politics were too heavy for your brain. You almost make me believe in reincarnation."

"I don't understand."

"Clearly, in another life you were Joan of Arc."

"Yes, you would like to see me burnt at the stake, wouldn't you? It would shut me up!"

"I cannot think of anything else that would," he said darkly.

"You are indeed right. Nothing will ever silence me. Politics concerns women as much as men. You ought to understand that but in some ways I think you are as bad as Lord Senwick. Yes, I want women to have the vote. Yes, I want to see us in Parliament and one day it will happen."

"I look forward to seeing that – "

"*Do not patronise me, sir.*"

"I didn't – "

"Yes, you did. I know that tone, the one that says 'here she goes again, dreaming impossible dreams.' But I only want women to be now able to defend themselves against unscrupulous men and I will do anything to achieve it. You, I think, would do anything to prevent it."

"That is grossly unfair – "

"Hah!"

"What does that mean?"

"It means hah!"

"It means you've run out of arguments," he said hotly. "When you've nothing left to say, sneer at your opponent. Great Heaven, Rosina! I would almost like to see you in a Parliamentary debate. You'd wipe the floor with some men I could think of."

"Now you are patronising me again."

"Can I say nothing right?" Sir John roared. "Rosina, I

admire your spirit, but there is still much that you don't understand."

"How convenient!" she scoffed. "How easy to simply say that and brush me aside."

"The man who could brush you aside would need to be very brave," said Sir John fervently. "He would also need to have a thick hide, and it would help if he was stone deaf."

She was strongly tempted to say "hah!" again, but she had a feeling that it would be unwise. Instead she turned away, intending to pace the floor. But then she stopped, transfixed by what she saw.

William Gladstone was standing in the doorway.

"Uncle William!" she exclaimed.

"My dear."

He embraced her warmly.

"Have you been there long?" she asked.

His granite face creased in a smile.

"Long enough for me to hear some very interesting comments. I had no idea you were such a firebrand. You are right about one thing. There have to be great changes in this country. Very great changes. And the time is coming."

Rosina gave Sir John a triumphant look.

"Then I can't wait for the election," she declared.

"Very soon now."

"Things are happening?"

"The Reform Bill has gone for the Royal Assent and then Disraeli can dissolve Parliament."

"But suppose he doesn't?"

"Then we'll just make him," replied Uncle William vigorously. "Now I have a great deal to discuss with your father."

"I will fetch him," she volunteered and hurried away.

She had a feeling that she had won her point in the game that pitched her and Sir John against each other.

But before she was out of earshot she heard Uncle William say,

"My god-daughter is indeed a really knowledgeable, intelligent young woman and just the perfect wife for you, John."

Then came Sir John's emphatic reply,

"I would as soon marry a buzzing gnat!"

This time she did say "hah!"

She said it to herself again when she had delivered the message to her father, and gone out into the garden.

She was not quite sure what she meant by it, but it made her feel better.

CHAPTER EIGHT

At last it was time to leave London. The election was under way in the new constituencies and with new voters.

Lord Blakemore's estate lay just within Sir Elroy's constituency and the family travelled to East Gradley on the same train as the Clarendons. Sir John came with them and spent most of his time talking to Lady Doreen.

"The factor that makes this election different to any other," he explained, "is that this country now has an extra one and a half million voters. Men owning land of a certain value, or even renting rooms of a certain value, can vote for the first time ever."

"But only men?" said Lady Doreen.

Sir John grinned.

"You must talk to Miss Clarendon about that. She has strong views on the subject, as indeed she has on every subject."

"As every woman should," declared Rosina firmly.

"Really ma'am?" he now teased her. "Only women? Surely we poor men are allowed strong opinions too?"

"I am sure that nobody could prevent them," she said, laughing reluctantly.

Later she drew Lady Doreen aside for a private talk.

"How are you feeling now?" she enquired. "You

always seem so cheerful on the surface that it makes me wonder if you are still hurt underneath."

"How kind you are," said her friend. "No, I am not hurting any more. My heart isn't broken. I don't think I really loved him. It is just that he seemed so different, a man from a background without privilege, determined to make his own way. I thought that was admirable. All I want now is to forget that I was on the point of making a fool of myself. Thank goodness you came to save me."

"Think no more of that!" said Rosina. "We are starting out on something new and exciting, which I think you will find absorbs your thoughts and your feelings so that you have no time to worry about anything else."

Lady Doreen laughed.

"I love the way you put it. I know I will enjoy being with you."

At East Gradley the two families left the train, while Sir John stayed on for the next stop, West Gradley.

Rosina stood on the platform waving as the train drew out. When it had gone the world felt very empty.

"Come along my dear," said her father. "We have work to do."

That evening he was visited by party officials. Both Rosina and her mother were present to hear the local party secretary tell him bluntly that his seat might be in danger.

"The part of the constituency that's been hived off to make South Gradley contained some of your most solid support," he explained. "And now most of the newly enfranchised men are in what is left of your territory. At this stage we simply don't know which way they will vote. We are all going to have to work very hard to make sure of them."

"What about Sir John Crosby next door?" Sir Elroy wanted to know. "Does he have the same problem?"

"Luckily, no. He has kept the safest part of his area and the new voters are mostly in the bit that's been assigned to the new constituency. There won't be any problem about returning him."

"Thank goodness!" said Sir Elroy. "He is coming over to help me, but I would hate to think he might be neglecting his own voters dangerously."

"Don't you worry, sir. Sir John is so popular that his party workers can do what is needed. It's right for him to help you. Just think, if you lost your seat when you were about to be made – "

"Not a word," said Sir Elroy quickly. "You mustn't talk or even think like that."

"That's understood, sir. But they're taking bets in the ale houses."

"If they must take bets on anything, tell them to bet on whether or not I get elected," said Sir Elroy, sounding harassed. "Nothing could be worse than letting people think I am taking success for granted."

Rosina had much to think about as she went to bed that night. The threat to her father was very real. He might lose his seat just as he was on the verge of gaining high political office.

'It mustn't happen,' she resolved fervently. 'Somehow Papa must win. If only Sir John arrives quickly tomorrow. I am sure he will know what to do.'

On that thought she fell asleep.

*

Sure enough Sir John was there early the following morning and with a plan of action already drawn up.

"I think we should start by visiting those people who can be found at home. After that we'll go to the factories. Many of the new voters are working men and that's where we'll find them."

Lady Clarendon came in and looked at her daughter proudly.

"I remember when I first went canvassing for your Papa," she said. "I was so thrilled. Now it's your turn."

"Do you have any good advice for me, Mama?"

"Don't forget that everyone has their own problems," replied Lady Clarendon. "You won't find anyone who doesn't have a problem of some sort."

Rosina nodded as her mother continued,

"Some are worried about their children, others are just anxious to elect someone who will help them with their own particular difficulties, whatever they may be."

"I suppose," suggested Rosina, "the majority of them want more money."

"Of course they do. No matter how much they have, they always feel poor, and would like to be better off. Which, I suppose, is also true of ourselves. Let them talk of their troubles, then be sympathetic and understanding. Leave them with a firm promise that if he is returned to Parliament, your father will do everything he can to make the people here as happy as possible."

"What about his opponent?" asked Rosina. "A Mr. Montague Rushley, I believe."

"He's a dreadful man," her mother scoffed at once. "Personally chosen by Disraeli for his 'oily' qualities. He's working very hard to do your father down by saying things about him which are untrue."

"How is he able to do that?" Rosina was shocked.

Lady Clarendon laughed.

"You know as well as I do that if someone wants something very important they lie and lie."

"Yes, I do," admitted Rosina, thinking of Arthur

Woodward.

"I am led to understand that Mr. Rushley's office has recently been joined by some very undesirable elements, men with no background or principles. At the moment it's all vague rumour and no certain details, but people have appeared who are unlike anyone we have dealt with before. They are hard and unscrupulous and now the constituency has been divided up, they see their chance."

"Well, we won't let them get away with it," insisted Rosina.

Sir Elroy came into the room. He was starting the journey with them on his way to a meeting of the election committee.

"Are you ready to go?" he asked.

"I was hoping Lady Doreen would have arrived by now," said Rosina, "but I suppose she won't. Maybe her father changed his mind."

"We can't wait for her," said Sir John. "There is so much to do."

So when Papa had gone to his meeting, it will just be herself and Sir John, Rosina thought, trying not to feel too pleased.

But just as they were leaving they saw a carriage approaching. When it came to a standstill, Lady Doreen climbed out.

"Here I am, ready to do all I can to help you," she said. "Did you think I had forgotten?"

"Not at all, it's lovely to see you," said Rosina, trying to feel glad. It would have been nice to have just one day alone with Sir John.

"Your servant ma'am," said Sir John, taking her hand and bowing over it.

"The more lovely girls to beguile the men into voting

for us, the better," came in Sir Elroy.

Lady Doreen laughed.

"My father was telling me at breakfast," she said, "that everyone in London is in a frenzy about this election. I am determined to work as hard as Rosina is doing."

"I am sure the two of you will be a great success," smiled Sir John.

"Thank you. I look forward to learning about other people's lives that are so different from our own," said Lady Doreen.

"I agree," Rosina concurred at once. "Think how much we can learn from the men who are working on the railways or down a coal mine. Also from women who have brought up a large number of children and have had to work in a shop or somewhere else to get the money to feed them. Mama insists that it's important to talk to the women too, even if they cannot vote, because they may influence their husbands."

"Do men ever listen to their wives?" queried Lady Doreen.

"I doubt it," Rosina said at once, "but that is Mama's theory."

"And she is quite right," added Sir Elroy. "I have always listened with deep respect to whatever my wife says, because she is such a wise woman."

Rosina laughed.

"It's all right, Papa. I promise to tell Mama that you said that."

"Thank you, my dear," sighed Sir Elroy, mopping his brow.

They all laughed at his relieved expression.

Having dropped Sir Elroy off at his meeting, the other three had an exhausting two hours talking with people who had only just gained the vote under the new bill and could still hardly believe it.

Rosina realised that it was going to be very hard making the men realise how important the election would be and how essential it was for them to vote the Liberal party into power. She talked about all the reforms Mr. Gladstone was planning that would improve their lives.

The men listened, but she was not quite sure how much they understood. When they finally emerged she said,

"Goodness, that was hard work. Do you think we did any good?"

"I hope we did," said Lady Doreen. "I thought you were brilliant in understanding how the election would affect them, when as far as I can make out they have never taken part in one before."

"We can only hope that something we have said to them will make them realise how much their vote matters."

"I never knew it could be so tiring having to repeat oneself endlessly," said Lady Doreen. "If I have to say again what I have already said fifty times, I think I will go mad."

"No you won't. You will go on working as we all do. Now here we are at the next place and it's time to say it all over again."

"You do it so well," sighed Lady Doreen. "I am trying to be as good as you, but I will fail, I know I will fail."

"You have to believe in yourself, just as you believe what we are telling them is the truth," answered Rosina. "They have been told a lot of lies by the opposition."

They stayed for an hour, talking earnestly and were both feeling exhausted when they came outside and climbed back into their carriage.

They were driving towards the next port of call and were passing the railway station, when Rosina gave a cry of joy.

"Stop! Stop!" she called to Wilkins, the coachman. "It's Charles."

Sure enough, there was her brother coming out of the station.

Wilkins pulled the horses to a standstill and Rosina opened the carriage door and jumped out.

"Charles! Charles!" she exclaimed. "How wonderful to see you again! Oh, my goodness, you're hurt."

To her horror she had noticed that his arm was in a sling.

He kissed his sister and then said,

"It's nothing serious. I fell down some stairs."

"But how did you come to do that?"

"Between you and me I had been making merry and – well, one thing led to another – "

"And you fell downstairs!"

"It was enough to get me some leave, so I thought I would come and help Papa win the constituency."

"I am so glad to see you," Rosina told him. "We're out canvassing. We can take you with us and you can go home afterwards."

"All right, if that is what you want," her brother agreed.

Seeing Sir John sitting in the carriage, Charles beamed with pleasure.

"I was hoping I'd find you here and in fact I tried to reach you before I left London and was told you were in the country."

"You have come home at exactly the right time," Sir John told him. "Things are very serious and we will all need to fight in every way we can to win what is likely to be a very unpleasant and a very violent battle."

"Good Heavens!" exclaimed Charles. "Is it as bad as that?"

"Worse," replied Sir John. "But let me introduce you to someone else who is helping your father, although I expect you will have met her before."

As he spoke Charles noticed the third person in the carriage and gave a cry.

"Doreen! How lovely to see you again. I didn't expect to find you here."

To Rosina's amusement she saw that he was blushing.

"I came to help the family work for your father," replied Lady Doreen. "I am so glad to see that you have come to do your duty."

"I think I am going to enjoy doing my duty now," he said smiling at her.

After Charles's luggage was piled onto the back of the carriage, they started off again.

They then visited three addresses in quick succession. Rosina and Lady Doreen left the last one first and waited in the carriage for a while before the men joined them.

"I never realised that there was so much work involved in politics," commented Lady Doreen. "I wonder how Lettice Holden will like it."

"Miss Holden?" echoed Rosina sharply.

She realised that she had almost forgotten the wealthy Lettice. It was a rude shock to be reminded of her now.

"You know how you and I have been longing to marry her off to Sir John," Lady Doreen said mischievously.

"Have we?" asked Rosina, who had no recollection of longing for any such thing.

"Of course. A rich wife will be of enormous benefit to him and I understand that it's almost settled between them."

"Nonsense!" said Rosina before she could stop herself. "If that were so he would have told me or at least my father."

"But perhaps delicacy prevented him," persisted Lady Doreen. "Any man naturally doesn't like to appear too confident until he has received a firm answer."

Rosina was very pale and suddenly she could hardly find the breath to ask the next question.

"Are you now telling me that Sir John has actually proposed to Miss Holden?"

Her heart was beating hard as she waited for the answer.

"I am not quite sure," Lady Doreen responded slowly. "Normally she confides in me, but recently, when I have asked her how advanced matters were between them, she merely giggles and simpers."

"Then she doesn't sound like the kind of wife he needs," said Rosina in a voice that she hoped did not shake. "A wife who giggled would drive him out of his senses."

"So I think myself. But, you know, if he has proposed, he is committed."

"Of course," came back Rosina, a little sharply. "If he *has* proposed."

"Well, I'm sure it's only a matter of time. Whenever I have seen them together they've seemed so happy. Every time they dance, she always seems to be laughing."

Rosina was silent, thinking back to the times she had danced with Sir John. She had never felt like laughing. Rather she had wanted to feel his hand tightening in the small of her back, drawing her closer so that she could feel his warm breath on her cheek.

She had wanted to look deep into his eyes and see them burning as they looked at her.

She had wanted to watch his mouth, and wonder how

it would feel if he kissed her.

But she had not wanted to laugh.

At this moment she felt that she might never laugh again.

"Rosina?"

She became aware that Lady Doreen was talking to her, as though from a great way off.

"I'm – sorry," she stammered, startled back to reality.

"I said the men are coming. Now we can be on our way."

They were approaching the carriage, laughing and slapping each other on the back.

Rosina was watching Sir John as if from a distance and it was as though she was seeing him for the first time. How handsome he was, how splendid with his laughing face, his air of confidence and vibrant masculinity!

How could any woman refuse his proposal?

And how could she herself have been so blind all this time?

By the time they had reached the carriage and climbed in, she was in command of herself again and able to ask,

"How did you get on?"

"Not too badly," answered Sir John. "But, if you want the truth, we'll have to work hard to make them believe that they need to have the Liberals in power."

"But we have to win," said Rosina. "For Papa's sake, we simply must."

He laid his hand over hers.

"Don't you worry. Everything will be all right."

How often had he done this before, carelessly? Now she felt as though his touch burned her.

She wanted to snatch her hand away.

She wanted to leave it in his forever.

At the next place they were heckled by a man who was obviously primed with some very difficult questions. But they answered them well, because they were fighting for what they believed in.

Charles was particularly impressive. At any rate, Lady Doreen seemed to think so.

At last they reached home eager for their lunch. As they sat down to eat, Sir John said,

"I feel as if I have climbed to the top of the highest mountain and fallen down the other side."

"I know exactly that same feeling," agreed Rosina. "I think we deserve a good meal, but we must eat it quickly, because there is still so much to do this afternoon."

"I think I worked harder this morning than I have worked for a long time," sighed Sir John. "All I can say about you two ladies is that you are magnificent. I would be seriously worried if you were working for the opposition!"

"The last man I was talking to tried hard to convert me into being a Conservative," said Rosina. "He promised that if I became one, I should have everything I might want and innumerable men kneeling at my feet!"

They all laughed and then her brother said,

"If you believe that nonsense, you will believe anything."

"Thank you, my brother dear! You are more than complimentary!"

"Oh, you know what I mean."

"Brothers are never very complimentary," added Lady Doreen wisely.

"Besides, Miss Clarendon doesn't need politics to get men kneeling at her feet," observed Sir John. "She has most of London there already."

Most, she thought, but not all. *Not you.*

Charles now greeted Sir John's pronouncement with brotherly scepticism.

"*Rosina*?" he cried. "Never!"

His sister kicked him under the table.

"Eat up," she ordered, ignoring his yelp. "We need strength to keep us going this afternoon."

Lady Doreen groaned.

"Do we really have to?" she asked.

"Of course we have to," Charles told her. "But I'll look after you and I promise you that you won't find it so tiring as you did at first."

Rosina and Sir John exchanged significant glances.

By the time they were able to cease work and enjoy a late tea, they all said they had never worked harder in their whole lives.

"And now," said Sir John, "I am going home to have a bath and to tell the truth I'm going to bed very early, because I'm exhausted."

Rosina laughed.

"Nonsense! You are enjoying every moment of it. I saw you this afternoon holding forth volubly to several women who were entranced by you."

"But how will that help?" Lady Doreen wanted to know. "After all, women don't have the vote, so what is the point of entrancing them?"

"There isn't one," said Rosina. "But Sir John enjoys female adulation. Since Miss Holden isn't here he has to make do with any he can find."

If she had hoped to surprise a reaction from him, she was disappointed. He merely grinned at her.

It was time for Lady Doreen to leave and Charles took

her to where her carriage was waiting.

"You mustn't let them tease you," he told her. "You were splendid and I thought you not only looked lovely, but what you said was brilliant."

"Was I really all right?" asked Lady Doreen. "I have always been interested in politics. In our house you have to be, but I wish I understood more."

"Then you must let me tell all you about it," suggested Charles. "I will enjoy that even more than I enjoy gaining yet another vote for the Liberals."

He spoke in a way which made Lady Doreen look at him with an expression in her eyes which was very moving.

She got into the carriage and Charles closed the door behind her.

"Goodbye until tomorrow," he said gently. "I will be counting every moment until we meet again."

He spoke very quietly so that the coachman did not hear.

Then he kissed Lady Doreen's hand. As she smiled at him she drove off.

He stood watching the carriage until it was out of sight.

Then almost reluctantly he turned and walked back into the house.

"You look cheerful," Sir John commented.

Charles hastily removed the vague smile from his face and walked on past them into the garden.

"Poor old fellow," muttered Sir John. "He's past praying for."

"You think that he and Lady Doreen – ?"

"Certain of it. He has the look of a man in love."

"How does a man in love look?" Rosina asked him

curiously.

"You should know. You have seen enough of them gazing at you like dying donkeys!"

"Just because a man looks like a dying donkey I don't think that means he's really in love," countered Rosina. "I am sure the real thing is something quite different."

"May I ask if you speak from experience, ma'am?"

"Well, nobody has ever seen me looking like a dying donkey."

"I believe you. You have far too much common sense."

She had never realised before that 'common sense' could be such a crushing phrase.

"I pride myself on my common sense," she retorted defiantly.

He gave her an ironic little bow.

"How wise of you. Now, it's time I was returning to my own home, so I will bid you good day."

As he walked to the front door Rosina followed him, unwilling to let him out of her sight until the last moment. She stood there wistfully as he went down the steps to his carriage.

Then she stiffened.

"I'll see you early tomorrow," he called back to her. "Rosina? Rosina, what is it?"

When she did not answer he came running back up the steps.

"What is it?" he repeated.

"Nothing, I – I thought I saw – "

"What did you see?" He took her arms gently and gave her a little shake. "Tell me."

"I thought I saw him, Arthur Woodward."

"Where?" he demanded sharply.

"There, by the gate. He's gone now."

He turned at once, racing back down the steps and heading for the gate, looking one way then another. At last he came back to her.

"There's nobody there."

"I might have imagined it, but I've seen him several times before."

Sir John drew her back into the house and closed the door.

"What do you mean, you have seen him before?" he asked urgently.

"I saw him twice in London. He stands so still and he glares at me with hate. I thought at first it was just my fancy, but he keeps coming back. Oh, John, I must be going mad."

"Nonsense," he soothed her reassuringly. "Of course you're not."

"Then why do I see a man who isn't there?"

"Perhaps he is. We know he hates you and blames you for his misfortunes. Maybe he's following you and trying to upset you. All the more reason for you to be careful."

She gave a shudder.

"Yes, I suppose so. But where is he? After what happened, he just seems to have vanished."

"And that's why he seems to come and go like a will'o the wisp," he agreed. "I will find him and when we can locate him in one place it will set your mind at rest."

"Can you do that?" she implored. "Oh, please."

"It may take a couple of days, but I'll track him down. I won't let anyone hurt or frighten you. Rosina, please don't worry."

She looked up at him, her heart glowing at the warmth

in his voice. She felt his hands on her shoulders, strong and reassuring, as though he would fight the entire world for her sake.

But then a cold wind swept over her as she recalled what Lady Doreen had said about Lettice Holden.

This man was virtually engaged to another woman.

Which meant that he could never be hers.

She should not be here with him, growing so close to him. From now on that feeling was forbidden.

She gave a horrified gasp and pulled away.

"Thank you," she murmured hurriedly. "I shall be most grateful for anything you can do for me. Now I will bid you goodnight."

"Goodnight," he said, giving her a puzzled look. "Rosina – "

"Goodnight, goodnight," she cried.

She almost ran away, but when she heard him close the door and go down the steps, she ran to the window and watched him get into his carriage.

She did not move until the carriage had swung out of the gate and vanished from sight.

Her eyes were full of tears.

He was lost to her.

CHAPTER NINE

Rosina lay awake most of that night, trying to collect her thoughts.

How could this have happened? How could she have understood that she loved John only now, when it was too late?

Of course the feelings had been there for a long time. She had always felt at ease with him, but she had assumed that it was no more than friendship.

But then, was not friendship also a key part of love? Would it not be wonderful to marry a man knowing that he was your friend as well as your lover?

She could talk to him as she could to nobody else. Even their frequent arguments were no more than a meeting of minds and she often enjoyed them.

Recently everything had changed. In his presence she had become aware of a new excitement. Dancing with him, feeling his arms hold her, his strong body moving close to hers, had thrilled her as nothing had ever done before.

And still she had refused to understand what was so plain and obvious.

She loved him.

Her girlish infatuation had given way to the passionate love of a woman, but it had happened when she was angry with him about Miss Draycott.

He had tried to warn her that Woodward could not be relied on, but she had misunderstood, thinking that he was siding with a villain, when he had only been trying to protect her from pain.

In her anger she had turned on him and so failed to comprehend her own feelings.

It was true as Lady Doreen had said. She had at least half encouraged him to court Lettice Holden, although she had done so in an ironic way. But he would not have understood that she was saying things she did not really mean.

Or perhaps he did not care what she meant? Perhaps he was really set on this wealthy match for the benefits it could bring him?

When she woke up in the morning, her pillow was wet with tears.

She braced herself to meet her family without letting them suspect that anything was wrong, but when she entered the breakfast room only her brother was present.

He did not seem to notice her air of strain, being too preoccupied with his own thoughts and Rosina became aware that he seemed full of suppressed excitement.

"Is something the matter?" she asked him.

"Nothing is wrong, but something is wonderful," he replied. "As soon as Mama and Papa come in, I'll tell you all about it."

"No, tell me now," she begged.

"All right. Last night, after we had returned home, I slipped out and rode over to Blakemore House. They were all about to go to bed when I arrived, but I managed to say everything I wanted to say."

He stopped. His face was shining with happiness.

"Is it – Lady Doreen?" asked Rosina.

"Yes," he said, beaming. "I asked Lord Blakemore for his permission to pay court to her and he agreed."

"What did she say?"

"Very little in words. She just smiled and nodded. We're not officially engaged, but I may court her with a view to becoming engaged soon."

"But – so soon?"

"It isn't soon for me. I have loved her from the moment we met at your debut ball. Since I have been apart from her I have thought of nothing else but her and how I could contrive another meeting."

"Did you really fall down those stairs?" teased Rosina.

"Well – I may not have tried very hard to save myself," he conceded with a sheepish grin. "I knew I had to get back on land and see her again. I never thought for a moment that I'd be lucky enough to win her. But she says that she likes me and could perhaps love me. That's all I dare to hope for at the moment."

"Oh, Charles, how wonderful! She is very dear to me and I am sure you could make each other very happy."

They hugged each other.

Rosina half thought she must be dreaming, but nothing could be more marvellous than for Charles to marry her friend.

At last her parents entered the breakfast room and Charles told his story again. They were overjoyed and for a while Rosina was able to join in their delight.

Then her happiness dimmed a little. It might have been herself and Sir John celebrating the future.

But it would not be, because she had thrown him into the arms of another woman.

Now she was faced with a long lifetime of regret, wondering how things might have turned out if she had known her own heart sooner. Perhaps she could have won him?

But she would never know.

"I daresay she will be here soon," said Sir Elroy. "It will be lovely to see her."

But Lady Doreen did not arrive and neither did Sir John.

Time wore on until it was well past the moment when they should both have arrived and everybody's heart sank.

"I'm going over to Blakemore Hall," Charles said at last. "Something must have happened."

"Wait!" cried Rosina, looking out of the window. "She's here. In fact, they are both arriving."

The two carriages were now drawing up together, one containing Lady Doreen and one with Sir John. Both of them were frowning and looking agitated.

They jumped out, greeted each other tensely and entered the house arm in arm.

"For pity's sake, what is it?" demanded Charles, going straight to Lady Doreen and taking her hands. "My darling, tell me everything."

"I hardly know how to," she said in a shaking voice. "Something has happened which – which – oh, Sir John, how can I tell you?"

"But how can it have anything to do with him?" Charles wanted to know.

"Early this morning a messenger arrived from London with devastating news. You may remember that my Papa wanted George to come here with us and George refused. Now we know why. He has eloped."

"*Eloped*?" echoed Charles. "But why should he need to? Surely anyone would welcome him as a son-in-law?"

"Yes, but Papa does not approve of the lady he has

chosen, so George ran off with her. He must have been planning it all this time and put his plan into action as soon as we had left London."

"But who has he eloped with?" Charles demanded.

"*Lettice Holden*," whispered Lady Doreen, her eyes on Sir John.

For a moment he did not react. He merely stared at her as if thunderstruck.

Rosina's eyes were fixed on his face, but she could not decide whether he was heart-broken or merely astonished.

"Did you say – Lettice Holden?" he asked at last.

"Yes, Sir John, I am afraid I did. I know that this news will come as a terrible blow to you – "

She got no further.

Sir John now threw back his head and began to laugh helplessly, while they all stared at him and Rosina felt a surge of happiness.

She could hardly believe what was happening.

"Forgive me," he said eventually. "I am not sure how you were expecting me to react but – " he shrugged, smiling.

"I think you are splendid," Lady Doreen told him fervently. "We were all sure that you and she would make a match of it. Indeed Rosina and I did everything we could to bring it about and it's so terrible that our efforts have all been in vain."

"I am indebted to Miss Clarendon – and you of course – for these efforts on my behalf," said Sir John in an ironic voice. "But it seems I was defeated by the better man!"

"Oh, such nonsense!" came back Lady Doreen with unexpected robustness. "George isn't the better man, just the poorer one. You see, she has a tremendous amount of money and George owes so much that he simply cannot afford to marry anyone else. Papa refused to countenance the match because he thinks she's vulgar, but he doesn't know the full extent of George's debts and George is too scared to tell him."

"What do the Holdens think of the match?" enquired Sir John.

"It seems they were in on the plot," said Lady Doreen crossly.

"Well, George is heir to an Earldom," muttered Sir John. "How can I compete?"

"Oh, Sir John, are you terribly disappointed?" asked Lady Doreen tragically.

Rosina held her breath and her heart suddenly beat wildly.

"Please don't you think of me as being in any way disappointed or dismayed," he replied. "In fact I feel I have had a lucky escape. Just think – if she couldn't capture any larger prey she might have set her sights on me."

He shuddered.

"But you seemed so happy together," protested Lady Doreen. "She was always laughing."

"Oh, heavens yes!" he groaned. "How that woman laughed! It was a dreadful sound, but it was better than her simpering. So I was just the stalking-horse for your brother? Never mind, I dare say I will just be able to bear the disappointment!"

He sounded somewhat light-hearted, Rosina thought, scarcely daring to believe what was happening.

He was free.

He did not belong to another woman.

But she must still be careful, as he had given no sign that he loved her.

Nevertheless, she refused to let anything dampen her soaring spirits. She could yet win his love.

It was some time before Rosina could get Sir John to herself. First the others must tell him their news and he must exclaim over it and congratulate the happy couple.

But at last Sir Elroy and his wife drew Lady Doreen and their son aside and Rosina was free to confront Sir John.

"Shame on you," she told him, "for speaking about Miss Holden like that. Clearly she married George on the rebound because you were so hard-hearted."

"But I was not," he said innocently. "I threw myself at her feet and offered my heart and soul if only she would give me the free run of her purse."

"Oh, *really*!" exclaimed Rosina indignantly.

"Why do you say that? Confess, Rosina, it was what you meant me to do. I am so sorry to disappoint you. I suppose she must have found something lacking in my declarations of undying love."

He gave a melancholy sigh that did not deceive her for a moment.

"You could have had the Holden fortune," she said, eyeing him askance.

"Yes, however will I manage without it? But I cannot help feeling that George needs it more than I do. In fact I think they may be very happy together."

"How can you say that? She is a thoroughly silly young woman."

"True. But then he is a thoroughly silly young man. Since neither of them is cursed with an excess of brains, they will suit each other together admirably."

Rosina was forced to admit that this was indeed possible.

"Brains do matter in a marriage," he added after a moment. "They matter more than you might think, almost as much as love. A couple cannot be happy if their minds are not in tune."

It was unnerving to hear her own thoughts of last night put into words, but at the same time exhilarating.

Was he trying to tell her something?

"Before the others came back, there's something I must say to you," he began.

"Yes?"

Her heart was beating faster.

"It's about Woodward."

"Oh," she said in a flat voice.

"I'm afraid you were right about him. He *is* here."

"Here in Gradley? I really did see him?"

"Almost certainly. But wait until I tell you the worst, the really incredible part of the story. Woodward has gone over to the other side!"

Her hands flew to her face.

"You mean – ?"

"He is now working for the Conservatives, helping Montague Rushley win this seat away from your father."

"Oh, no! How could he? He is a Liberal. He believes in our cause."

"I am afraid a man like that believes in nothing except what will serve to advance himself. One side or the other, it's all one to him."

"And he'll really try to harm Papa? It's all my fault. Oh, what have I done?"

"Rosina, this is not your fault. You must not believe that."

"But if Papa loses the seat, I shall blame myself for the rest of my days."

"Then we must make sure that he doesn't lose it. From now on we must think of nothing else but the election."

"Yes," she agreed with a little sigh. "Nothing else."

She would just have to be patient, she told herself. Between now and the election they would have plenty of time together.

She soon realised that Sir John had been right to warn her about Woodward's activities. She did not see him, but she was always aware of him working behind the scenes. At meetings there was always one determined heckler, very well primed with hard questions. Too well primed for it to be an accident.

*

But she never saw Arthur Woodward himself and slowly time moved on until it was almost the day of the election.

She was out doing some last minute canvassing on her own, accompanied only by Wilkins, the coachman who had been with the family for twenty years.

She felt satisfied with her day's work. She had done her best and now there was nothing more she could do to help her father.

Rosina was walking towards the carriage which was waiting for her, when she suddenly realised that there was a familiar figure on the other side of the road.

It was Arthur Woodward.

He was just coming out of a small shabby house and it seemed to her that there was something furtive in his manner.

He turned sharply to the right and began walking down the street at a determined pace, as if it was important for him to reach somewhere quickly.

On an impulse Rosina stood up on the seat of the carriage which was open and ordered Wilkins,

"Follow that man who is walking along the pavement and keep well behind him because I wish to know where he is going."

Wilkins chuckled.

"What are you up to now, Miss Rosina?" he asked.

"He is a bad and wicked man," answered Rosina, "and I want to know what he is doing, because I am sure it's something deceitful and underhand. As he is walking on the pavement, he won't realise we are just behind him."

Wilkins chuckled again.

But because he was used to the odd things the children of his employer had done ever since he had driven them, he obeyed Rosina's command, moving slowly so that Arthur Woodward was well in front.

Then suddenly he stopped and turned towards a house on the left side. Pushing open the door he went in and disappeared.

The coachman brought the carriage to a standstill.

"Now what do you want me to do, Miss Rosina?"

"I am just wondering what that man is up to. He's done everything in his power to prevent Papa from getting the votes he wants and I would like to know what he is doing in that house."

There was silence for a moment and then Wilkins said,

"It may be untrue, but I was told when I was having a drink at an ale house nearby that the other side are printing a lot of extra voting slips."

Rosina drew in her breath sharply.

"False voting slips!" she exclaimed.

"So they said and then they fill them in to make sure Montague Rushley wins. I wondered if I should tell your father, but then I thought it would only worry him and perhaps it were a lie."

Rosina thought, although she did not say so, that ten to one it was true and Arthur Woodward was up to making

135

mischief again, as ruthless and dishonest in one way as he had been in another.

"Let us wait for a moment," Rosina decided, "and when he comes out, I'll call at the house and see what's happening inside."

"Just you be careful, miss. I'm not having you get into trouble over what I've told you. The Master would skin me alive."

"I'll be careful," Rosina promised. "But I have to find out and put a stop to it, if it's what we think. It will break Papa's heart if he is thrown out after so many years of helping the people here."

Wilkins pulled the horses up beside a large tree on the opposite side of the road to the house.

Ten minutes passed.

Rosina was just beginning to think perhaps it was a waste of time when the door opened and the man she hated came out.

Without noticing them, because they were on the other side of the road and behind a large tree, Arthur Woodward turned and walked quickly away.

As soon as he was out of sight, Rosina said,

"I must find out what he has been doing. Suppose I go to the back door and see who's inside."

"It's best if I do that," replied Wilkins. "You stay here with the horses."

He took off his hat, put it on the floor of the carriage and strode off muttering,

"The things I do for this family!"

Rosina slipped into his seat and held the reins while he walked across the road and disappeared into the back of the house.

She sat waiting, wondering if she was allowing her

imagination to run away with her. Surely there was nothing in the house which could possibly endanger her father?

'Perhaps I am being stupid and wasting time,' she told herself. 'But Arthur Woodward is unpleasant and dangerous. I must protect Papa in every way I can.'

Wilkins was away for quite a long time. When he came back Rosina knew even before he spoke from the expression on his face that he had found something.

As he reached the carriage he looked to the right and left, as if to make sure that no one was listening or watching them.

Then he said,

"We were quite right, Miss Rosina, that man is up to no good."

"What is happening?"

"Well, as far as I can make out, miss, they're forging a great number of voting slips. In fact there's a pile of them on the table in the sitting-room. Luckily the man who was there left the room for a moment and I slipped in and grabbed a few. Here."

He showed her the papers in his hand and Rosina drew in her breath sharply at what she saw. They were indeed false voting slips and every one had been filled in for Montague Rushley.

"Well done, Wilkins!" she exclaimed. "Let's get home quickly and show my father."

"I'll do that right enough, miss," said Wilkins, as he climbed into his seat.

"Papa is going to be very grateful to you for this, Wilkins."

She was right.

Her father was fervent in his thanks to his faithful servant. Sir John was horrified and angry.

"Let's hurry back with the police," asserted Sir Elroy. "The sooner Woodward is behind bars the better." He patted Rosina's hand. "Don't worry, my dear. We'll soon be back."

"I'm coming with you, Papa."

"Certainly not. It's no place for a woman."

"It was a woman who discovered this outrage," she replied. "And I want to be in at the kill."

"Let her come with us," suggested Sir John. "This is Rosina's triumph and she now has the right to see it to a conclusion."

His eyes met hers as he spoke and she knew he was saying that he understood why she would want to be present at the downfall of Arthur Woodward.

She smiled and held out her hand in gratitude and he squeezed it, smiling back at her.

"Well, if you think so," said Sir Elroy dubiously.

A footman was despatched to the local Police Station and half an hour later a man arrived in plain clothes, who introduced himself as Detective Inspector Vanner. He had a uniformed Constable with him.

"We've suspected this for some time," he told Sir Elroy, "but we could never be certain of the headquarters. If your information is correct, sir, you've performed a valuable service to the community."

"Let's go and catch them red-handed," said Rosina urgently.

The detective also looked askance at the idea of a lady going with them, but Sir John backed her up and Sir Elroy said nothing to the contrary.

He merely looked at the two of them with curiosity and pleasure.

He was a very perceptive man.

Darkness was falling as they set out and went to the

end of the street where the house stood.

There they halted.

"It's the third house on the left," Rosina told the detective. "You cannot see any lights from the front because they are working around the back."

They all crossed the road, went quietly in through the gate and made their way around the side of the house to where a staircase led down to the basement. From here they could just see a light.

"Please wait here," said the detective, signalling to the constable to follow him.

The two Policemen now descended to the basement, followed by Sir Elroy and Sir John.

Rosina stayed behind, listening to the silence that seemed to go on forever. Then came a mighty crash as the door was kicked in, followed by shouts.

Unable to bear the suspense any longer she crept down the stairs and saw the men fighting behind the windows. There was Arthur Woodward and another man, struggling in the arms of the law.

Delighted, Rosina ran down the stairs.

"We've got them, miss," trumpeted the detective. "Now then, you – " he was talking to Arthur Woodward, "you've got some explaining to do and you'll do it at the Police Station."

"You can't treat me like this," Woodward bawled. "I am an important man."

"No," intervened Rosina, "you could have been an important man, if you hadn't been eaten up by pride and greed."

He looked at her with venom.

"*You!*" he said with loathing. "I owe all my misfortune to you."

She regarded him evenly.

"I hope so. I really hope so."

That was too much for him. Wrenching himself free from the Constable he launched himself on Rosina.

He landed hard enough to carry her down to the floor.

The next moment she felt his hands at her throat, squeezing the life out of her.

CHAPTER TEN

For a terrible moment everything went black. Rosina fought and kicked, but the man holding her was enraged to the point of being a maniac and she could not move him.

His hands were growing tighter around her throat and she was losing consciousness.

Then, just when she thought everything was over, the weight crushing her vanished. Rough hands now hauled Woodward to his feet and slammed him back against the wall with a violent curse.

"John – " she gasped weakly. "John – "

He did not seem to hear her. Fear for her safety and fury at her attacker had transformed Sir John. She caught a glimpse of his face as her father helped her to her feet and could hardly recognise him.

His face was savage with hatred for anyone who would dare to hurt her.

For a terrible moment she dreaded that he might kill Woodward.

And she did not want that for the harm it would do to John himself. She did not want him standing trial. She wanted him free and safe to live his life.

And to marry her.

"John," she screamed. "Let him go, *please*."

But all his concentration was on Woodward, whose eyes bulged from his head and his face was distorted by fear.

"Don't you dare lay a hand on her," Sir John grated. "Or I'll kill you. Do you understand me?"

"Now then, sir," interposed Detective Vanner. "Let him go. I'll deal with him from now on."

But Sir John did not move. His hands seemed frozen to Woodward's neck and there was murder in his eyes.

But then Rosina laid her hand on his arm.

"Let him go," she begged him. "Don't you see, it's time to think only of us. Don't let him spoil that."

Her words reached him as nothing else could have done.

Slowly he relaxed and allowed her to pull him away. He was breathing hard.

"That's right, sir. I don't want to have to arrest you as well, do I? What would the young lady say to that?"

Detective Vanner gave a sly look at Rosina, who suddenly blushed.

Sir John turned his head and looked at her intently.

"Now let's get back to business," the Policeman said. "Look at these."

He was pointing at the table. "All these false ballots slips made out against you, Sir Elroy. Probably enough to deny you the seat, if they'd been put into the system."

"And look here, sir," added the Constable, "all this money. Looks like counterfeit to me."

Detective Vanner surveyed Arthur Woodward.

"You'll be going away for a very long stretch, my lad. Right, come along with you."

He hauled him away, while the Constable took away the other man.

"My, that was exciting," bubbled Sir Elroy, brushing himself down. "Thank Heavens he has been defeated. To think of him daring to attack you, my dear. John, you have all my gratitude for what you did. I thought that fiend was going to kill Rosina."

"He would have liked to," mumbled Rosina.

"Thank goodness John was here to protect you. Fancy that."

"I am extremely grateful to Sir John, Papa."

"Well, I expect you would like to tell him so yourself. I'll be waiting for both of you in the carriage."

Sir Elroy departed quickly, leaving them looking at each other awkwardly.

"It was very brave of you to come to my rescue," murmured Rosina. "You have all my thanks."

She fell silent wondering what was happening.

Sir John was looking at her with a heart rending expression on his face and she no longer knew what to say to him. Her own heart was suddenly beating fast.

"It wasn't brave at all, Rosina, I could not bear you to be hurt. I would give my life for you."

She looked at him and his face still bore the same look that pierced her heart. It seemed to promise so much and yet she might be mistaken.

He might not really care for her at all and she knew that if John did not love her, then nothing else in the world mattered.

"John," she whispered, "Oh, John – "

He was beside her in an instant.

"Rosina – Rosina, my darling. Oh, my dearest love. Do you think you could love me?"

"*Yes*," she cried ecstatically. "Oh, indeed, yes, I could. I do. I've always loved you, but then I became angry with you and I told myself I didn't love you, but that wasn't really true. In my heart you were always there. But then I thought you were courting Miss Holden."

"And I thought you were trying to ensnare George Blakemore. I was wildly jealous, but what could I say?"

Then came the moment she had dreamed of, the magic moment when his arms closed around her body and he drew her close and kissed her.

The feel of his lips on hers made her feel that she was in Heaven. All the troubles and problems seemed to fall away simply because she was in the arms of the man she loved.

"My love, my love," he murmured against her lips. "I have loved you for months, but I couldn't tell you so. You were so young and I knew I must wait until you had a chance to look around you and make a better match."

"There is no better match than you," she told him passionately.

"I do not possess a great title like some of your suitors or a great fortune."

"Do you love me?"

"*With all my heart and soul, for ever and ever.*"

"Then you are a splendid match," she cried. "I will have no one but you."

"My darling!"

He embraced her again, fiercely this time, and she could sense all the passion that he had striven so long to hide.

"Let us leave this place," he said at last. "It's dark and full of hate and evil. For us there will be only light from now on."

She placed her hand in his and together they danced up the steps to where the coach was waiting.

"But where is Papa?" asked Rosina.

Wilkins leaned down from his box and winked at her.

"Sir Elroy took a cab home. He said he thought you'd enjoy having the coach to yourself."

"Wicked Papa!" exclaimed Rosina. "He was always determined to bring us together."

They climbed in and closed the door behind them. It was dark inside and there was no one to see the fervour of their embrace or listen to their whispered words of love.

"I must confess," admitted Sir John, "that I contrived it so that I should stay at your house. Otherwise I would hardly have seen you and I wanted to be there all the time, seeing you every day. I thought it would give me a chance to win your love."

"You didn't need to win it, I have loved you for a long time, but I thought you only saw me as a little girl."

"I had to fight not to tell you of my feelings. It would have been wrong to speak of them sooner, but now I am free to say that I love you and I shall love you forever."

He kissed her fiercely and she responded with ardour, rejoicing that they had finally found each other.

"My darling," he said to her at last, "is Miss Draycott laid to rest now?"

"Yes and I should never have let her come between us, but I was so angry with you when you seemed hard and unsympathetic to her plight."

"I never meant to sound like that, but her hopes and dreams seemed to me so unrealistic, when seen against the cruel world I knew, the world of men set on advancement at any cost to others. I meant only to utter a warning and I certainly did not intend to imply that I approved of creatures like Woodward."

"I just wouldn't listen to reason, would I?" she murmured. "I blamed you, wrongly."

"You spoke out of your generous heart and I love you more for it. I am so sorry that she couldn't be saved."

"But we did her justice in the end and for that we must be grateful. I suppose it was unwise of me to speak to that man as I did."

"Most unwise," he said lovingly. "But it was all part of your loyalty to your friend. I would not have you any different."

"But from now on I will be discreet for the sake of poor Miss Draycott. Sometimes I even hope that she is happy and content in Heaven."

"I am sure she is. You have done all you could for her and now you must let her rest."

"Yes," agreed Rosina. "I shall never forget her or cease to be grateful to her for showing me the truth about that man, so that I was able to help Lady Doreen. But now – "

"But now," he sighed, taking her into his arms, "now we may think about ourselves and the life that we shall make together."

He kissed her fervently and for the rest of the journey home, she rested her head contentedly on his shoulder.

When the coach drew up at their front door, they realised that someone was drawing back the curtains to watch them. Quickly the curtains were dropped back into place.

"I think that was Papa," said Rosina. "I know he has always wanted this, but whatever will Mama say?"

"Let's go and find out," suggested Sir John.

As they mounted the steps the door was pulled open by the butler and inside stood Sir Elroy and his lady, both beaming with expectation.

"Well?" queried Papa. "Well?"

"Oh, Papa!" cried Rosina. "I am so happy."

She ran into his arms and hugged him exuberantly. He in turn hugged her until she was breathless, delighted by the fulfilment of his dearest hope.

When she emerged from his embrace, she saw that her mother was also hugging John, and saying,

"My dear boy, I was afraid it would never happen."

"Mama?" she cried. "But you didn't want me to marry John."

"Nonsense, child, of course I did. But you've always been such a contrary creature that I knew if you thought I approved of him you would go the other way just to be difficult. So I ordered you not to think about him and I knew it would work."

"Mama! However could you be so conniving and duplicitous?"

"It was easy, my dear," her mother chuckled. "I simply wanted to see you happy and I knew the way to make it happen. Of course John is the man for you."

"Hush ma'am, begged Sir John, his eyes twinkling. "If you say any more she'll throw me over."

"I just wouldn't let her," declared Lady Clarendon, advancing on him with her arms wide.

Rosina watched, smiling, as they embraced and then her father shook his hand.

Now, she felt, he was really part of the family.

Next Charles arrived home having spent the day with the Blakemores and at first he was angry that he had missed all the fun, but when he heard what his sister had to tell him he was overjoyed and pumped John's hand eagerly.

Nobody wanted to go to bed as they were all far too excited by the day's events, but at last it was time for Sir John to go home.

They spent a last few precious minutes together.

"I don't want to leave you," he whispered. "I cannot bear to go away even though I know I will see you again tomorrow."

"Come back soon," she begged. "The time will seem so long without you."

"I love you," he told her tenderly. "I love you, I love you."

She went to the door and watched as his carriage rumbled out of the gate.

Then she went to bed and dreamed of him all night.

*

When Rosina awoke the following morning, she could hardly believe that everything was really happening.

Could it really be true that Sir John was in love with her? Just as she had been in love with him for such a long time, but she had thought it was something which would never be a part of reality.

'I love him! I love him,' she said to herself. 'I thank God a thousand times that he loves me.'

She thanked God that she could give him her whole heart without reserve.

'Nothing could be more wonderful,' she thought as she dressed. 'I have been so lucky to find John and I know when we are married, we will be so happy that we will somehow in some way make other people happy too.'

She dressed herself hurriedly because she wanted to go downstairs and see the man she loved.

She found him already there in the garden, having arrived early because he was so anxious to be with her.

She saw him walking across the lawn and felt a little throb in her heart, because not only was he there, but in the sunshine he was looking so handsome and so happy, just as she was so happy.

She ran out into the garden and threw herself into his arms, which folded possessively around her.

A few minutes later Lady Doreen arrived. Rosina saw her brother's joy at the sight of her and thought that the Almighty had been very kind to all of them.

The four of them then spent a happy day together. Officially they were canvassing, but not very much work was done as they were all too happy in each other's company.

And then, at last, it was the day of the election. Sir John called in on his way to the railway station to start the journey to his constituency.

"How much I should like to stay here to see your father voted back in," he told Rosina. "But I must be present for my own count."

"And Rosina should be by your side," commented Sir Elroy, coming into the hall in time to hear the conversation.

"But Papa, don't you want me with you?"

"Of course I do, but I'll have your mother and Charles and the Blakemores. You are going to be the wife of a Member of Parliament and it's right that the constituency should get its first view of you at his side for his great moment."

"He's right, my dearest," said Sir John. "It would mean the world to me."

"Oh, John, how I would love to be there with you."

"Hurry then, we leave in a few minutes."

Papa and Mama went with them to the station and waved them off. In half an hour they had crossed the constituency border into West Gradley and a few minutes later the train pulled into the station, where they were greeted by the party representatives.

Wherever they went, the announcement of their

engagement was greeted with joy.

Rosina's heart soared. She was marrying the man she loved and allying herself to the only life she wanted – all in one.

Together they travelled around the polling stations meeting some of the newly enfranchised men who had come to cast their first votes. They congratulated them and were congratulated in turn.

In the evening there was dinner at party headquarters and then on to the Town Hall for the count. As soon as they entered there were loud cheers and someone shouted,

"Well done, Sir John. They've just finished counting and you've won by three to one. The announcement will be made at any moment."

Then Rosina had the proud experience of standing beside her future husband on the balcony of the Town Hall, as he was announced the winner for the constituency of West Gradley to the cheering of the crowds below.

"If only things are going as well for Papa," she whispered to Sir John when they were inside. "I have been thinking of him and hoping he is all right."

"Don't worry," said Sir John. "You stopped Arthur Woodward's tricks and he is surely safe."

He looked at the clock.

"It's time we were leaving or we'll miss the last train and we must be there for your father's celebrations."

They made their farewells and set off. In less than an hour they were in East Gradley and at the station they took a cab to the Town Hall, where they found a crowd standing outside with an air of expectancy.

"They don't seem to have made an announcement yet," observed Sir John.

"That's right," someone called. "They're on the third

recount. It's very close."

They hurried inside and found Sir Elroy calmly drinking champagne surrounded by his family.

"Papa, this just cannot be happening," cried Rosina imploringly.

"Patience, my dear. I am ahead by only ten votes, but in three recounts they haven't managed to make that figure any less."

"Oh, goodness!" she breathed. "If they do manage it I think I will jump from the window and run away."

"If you do so I'll run after you," Sir John told her.

She slipped her hand into his.

"I am now so frightened that we have anticipated too much."

"Have faith, my love."

Even as Sir John spoke there was the sound of loud voices coming nearer. The Town Clerk appeared and stood before Sir Elroy.

"Congratulations," he announced. "Your opponent has conceded and you are the elected member for this constituency.

Lady Clarendon threw herself into her husband's arms. Rosina and John hugged eagerly, so did Charles and Lady Doreen.

Together they all went out onto the balcony and the Mayor made the declaration to the waiting crowds below. They cheered and cheered and cried aloud,

"*You have won*! *You have won*!"

As his family joined him, the voices grew even louder and Sir Elroy held up his hands and the cheers died away and there was silence.

"I want to thank you a thousand times for all your support and your help. What we have to do now is to make this country even greater than it is already."

He paused for a moment and there was a cheer, which he acknowledged with a wave, before continuing,

"God bless you all and thank you once again."

As he finished speaking there was a roar of applause.

Sir Elroy turned back into the room and said,

"Let us hope we're not rejoicing too soon and that Gladstone has the majority everyone predicts."

In the early hours they left the Town Hall and went to the Railway Station to catch the first train to London. Then they went straight to Party Headquarters, which they found in uproar.

"The results are coming in thick and fast," a man said. "It looks as though the Liberals are headed for a majority of over a hundred. And there's a message for you, Sir Elroy, from Mr. Gladstone. Will you please see him at five o'clock this afternoon? It's about what he had discussed with you earlier."

"What did he discuss with you, Papa?" Rosina wanted to know.

"Which position he plans to offer me, my dear. He gave me a choice of two, and I said I would think it over and let him know when he became Prime Minister."

"What are they, Papa? And which will you choose?"

But Sir Elroy put his finger to his lips.

"Do you know, Mama?" Rosina asked her mother who was just behind them.

"Oh, yes, your father told me weeks ago. He wanted me to help him decide."

"Then *tell*."

But she too shook her head and moved away, arm in arm with her husband. For the first time Rosina realised the full extent of the bond between them. Lovers and friends.

He would confide in her what he would tell to nobody else.

"You are very pensive, my darling," Sir John remarked tenderly. "Are you not happy?"

"Oh, yes, very happy. It's just that I am thinking about something you said, when Lord Blakemore managed to blight Arthur Woodward's chances merely by withdrawing his support. You said that it wasn't right that one man could ruin another man's political opportunities merely because the first man was powerful.

"I was angry because Woodward was so clearly a villain. But I have realised that you were right. It would have made no difference if he hadn't been a villain. Once a powerful man like Lord Blakemore became his enemy, his chance would be over. And it is wrong that one man should have so much power."

Sir John nodded.

"Thank Heavens I am marrying a lady who can think for herself," he said. "This is a fine and splendid country, but there's still much that should be put right – like some people having too much power and others too little.

"Today we have taken the first step by giving so many more people the vote and encouraging them to use it. Now we must look forward to the next step and the one beyond. And I thank my stars that I shall have you beside me."

"And I shall stay beside you forever, because this is the only place I want to be."

Rosina rested her head on his shoulder, happy in her love and happier still in the true meeting of their minds.

Sir John's words, *thank Heavens I am marrying a lady who can think for herself*, seemed to shine a light before her, illuminating the years ahead when they would grow closer and more united not only in heart, but in mind and soul.

And that was all she asked out of life.